THE BABY SMURF

Peyo

THE BABY SMURF

Hey! Here's a gift for you!
I don't understand...! Maybe Smurfette...
BAM
WAAAAAHH!
Oh!
A BABY!
Arhoo...
COME, EVERYONE! COME SEE THE BABY SMURF!
Beleb!
Peyo
2

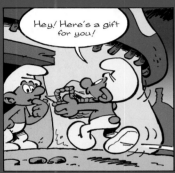

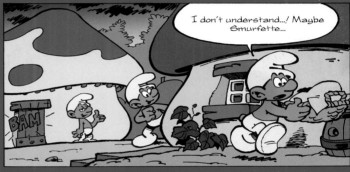

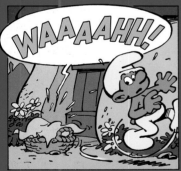

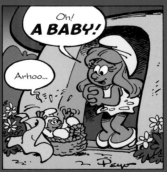

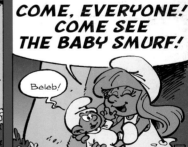

A SMURFS GRAPHIC NOVEL BY Peyo

PAPERCUTZ™
NEW YORK

SMURFS GRAPHIC NOVELS AVAILABLE FROM PAPERCUTZ™

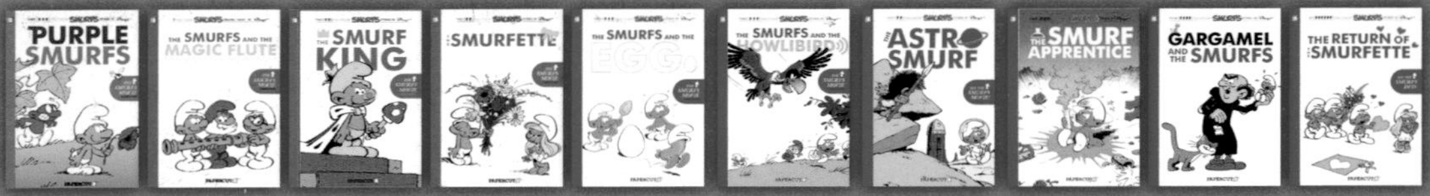
PURPLE SMURFS
THE SMURFS AND THE MAGIC FLUTE
THE SMURF KING
SMURFETTE
THE SMURFS AND THE EGG
THE SMURFS AND THE HOWLIBIRD
ASTRO SMURF
THE SMURF APPRENTICE
GARGAMEL AND THE SMURFS
THE RETURN OF THE SMURFETTE

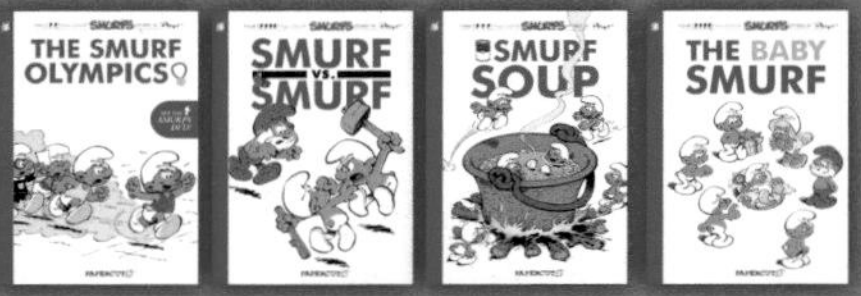
THE SMURF OLYMPICS
SMURF VS. SMURF
SMURF SOUP
THE BABY SMURF

1. THE PURPLE SMURFS
2. THE SMURFS AND THE MAGIC FLUTE
3. THE SMURF KING
4. THE SMURFETTE
5. THE SMURFS AND THE EGG
6. THE SMURFS AND THE HOWLIBIRD
7. THE ASTROSMURF
8. THE SMURF APPRENTICE
9. GARGAMEL AND THE SMURFS
10. THE RETURN OF THE SMURFETTE
11. THE SMURF OLYMPICS
12. SMURF VS. SMURF
13. SMURF SOUP
14. THE BABY SMURF

COMING SOON:

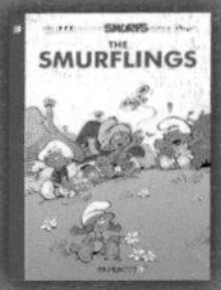
THE SMURFLINGS

15. THE SMURFLINGS

THE SMURFS graphic novels are available in paperback for $5.99 each and in hardcover for $10.99 each at booksellers everywhere. You can also order online at www.papercutz.com. Or call 1-800-886-1223, Monday through Fridays, 9 – 5 EST. MC, Visa, and AmEx accepted. To order by mail, please add $4.00 for postage and handling for first book ordered, $1.00 for each additional book and make check payable to NBM Publishing. Send to: Papercutz, 160 Broadway, Suite 700, East Wing, New York, NY 10038.

THE SMURFS graphic novels are also available digitally wherever e-books are sold.

WWW.PAPERCUTZ.COM

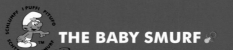

THE BABY SMURF

"The Baby Smurf"
BY PEYO

"A Smurfing Party"
BY PEYO

"The Weather-Smurfing Machine"
BY PEYO WITH GOS

"The Red Taxis"
A BENNY BREAKIRON PREVIEW
BY PEYO (WITH BACKGROUNDS BY WILL)

Joe Johnson, *SMURFLATIONS*
Adam Grano, *SMURFIC DESIGN*
Janice Chiang, *LETTERING SMURFETTE*
Matt. Murray, *SMURF CONSULTANT*
Michael Petranek, *ASSOCIATE SMURF*
Jim Salicrup, *SMURF-IN-CHIEF*

PAPERBACK EDITION ISBN: 978-1-59707-381-3
HARDCOVER EDITION ISBN: 978-1-59707-382-0

PRINTED IN CHINA FEBRUARY 2013 BY WKT CO. LTD.
3/F PHASE I LEADER INDUSTRIAL CENTRE
188 TEXACO ROAD, TSEUN WAN, N.T., HONG KONG

DISTRIBUTED BY MACMILLAN
FIRST PAPERCUTZ PRINTING

THE SMURF BABY

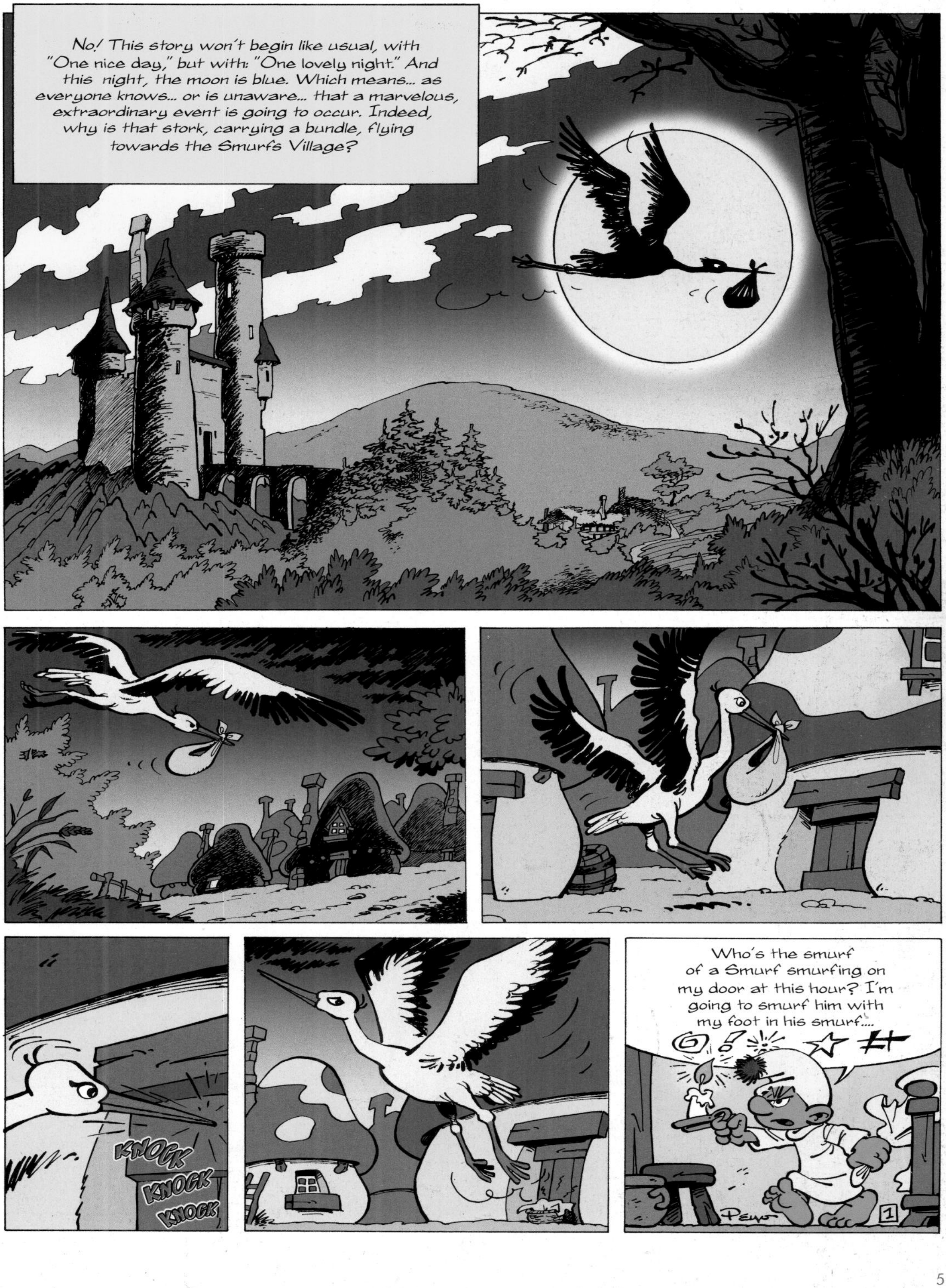
No! This story won't begin like usual, with "One nice day," but with: "One lovely night." And this night, the moon is blue. Which means... as everyone knows... or is unaware... that a marvelous, extraordinary event is going to occur. Indeed, why is that stork, carrying a bundle, flying towards the Smurfs Village?
KNOCK
KNOCK
KNOCK
Who's the smurf of a Smurf smurfing on my door at this hour? I'm going to smurf him with my foot in his smurf....

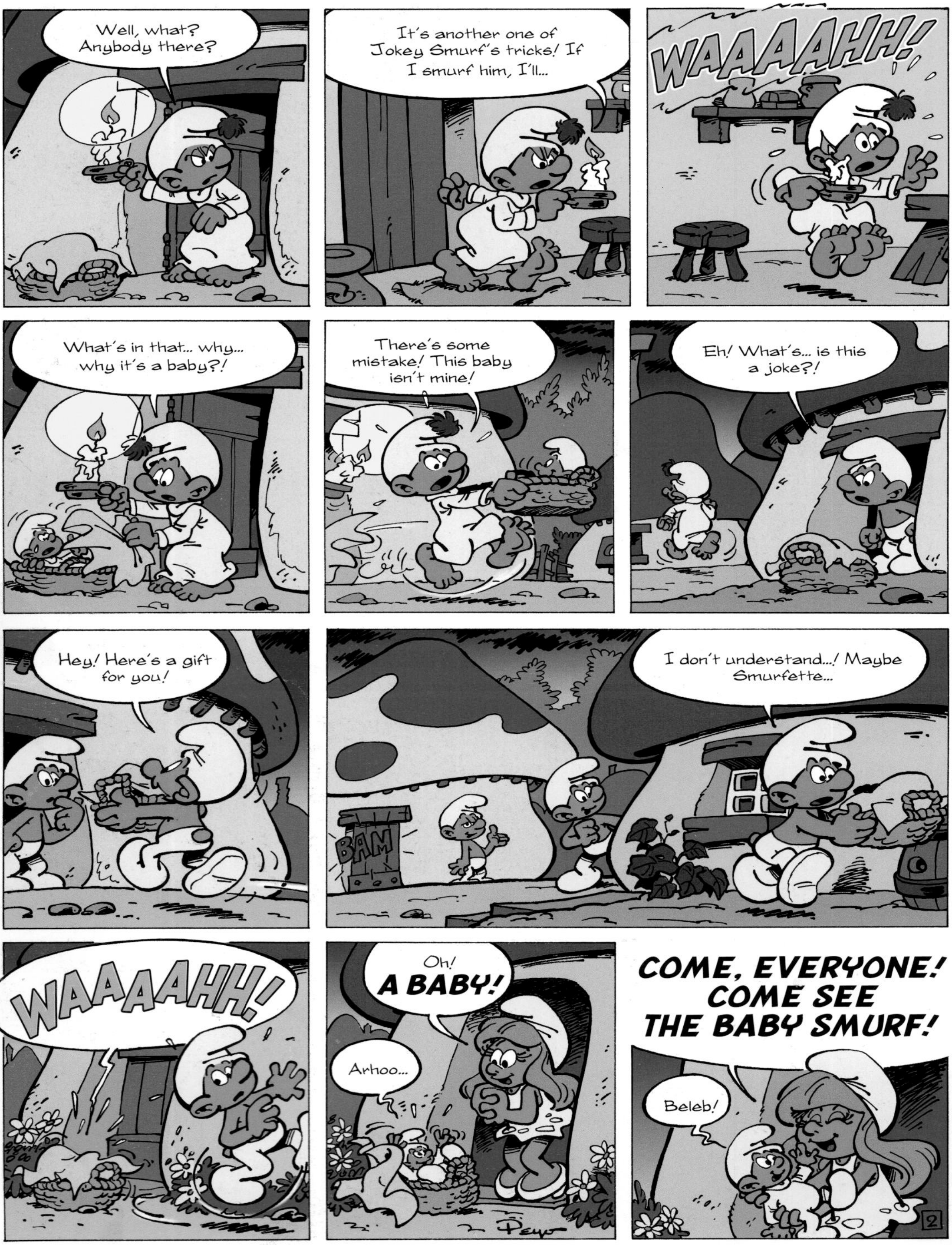

Well, what? Anybody there?
It's another one of Jokey Smurf's tricks! If I smurf him, I'll...
WAAAAAHH!
What's in that... why... why it's a baby?!
There's some mistake! This baby isn't mine!
Eh! What's... is this a joke?!
Hey! Here's a gift for you!
I don't understand...! Maybe Smurfette...
BAM
WAAAAHH!
Oh! A BABY!
Arhoo...
COME, EVERYONE! COME SEE THE BABY SMURF!
Beleb!
2

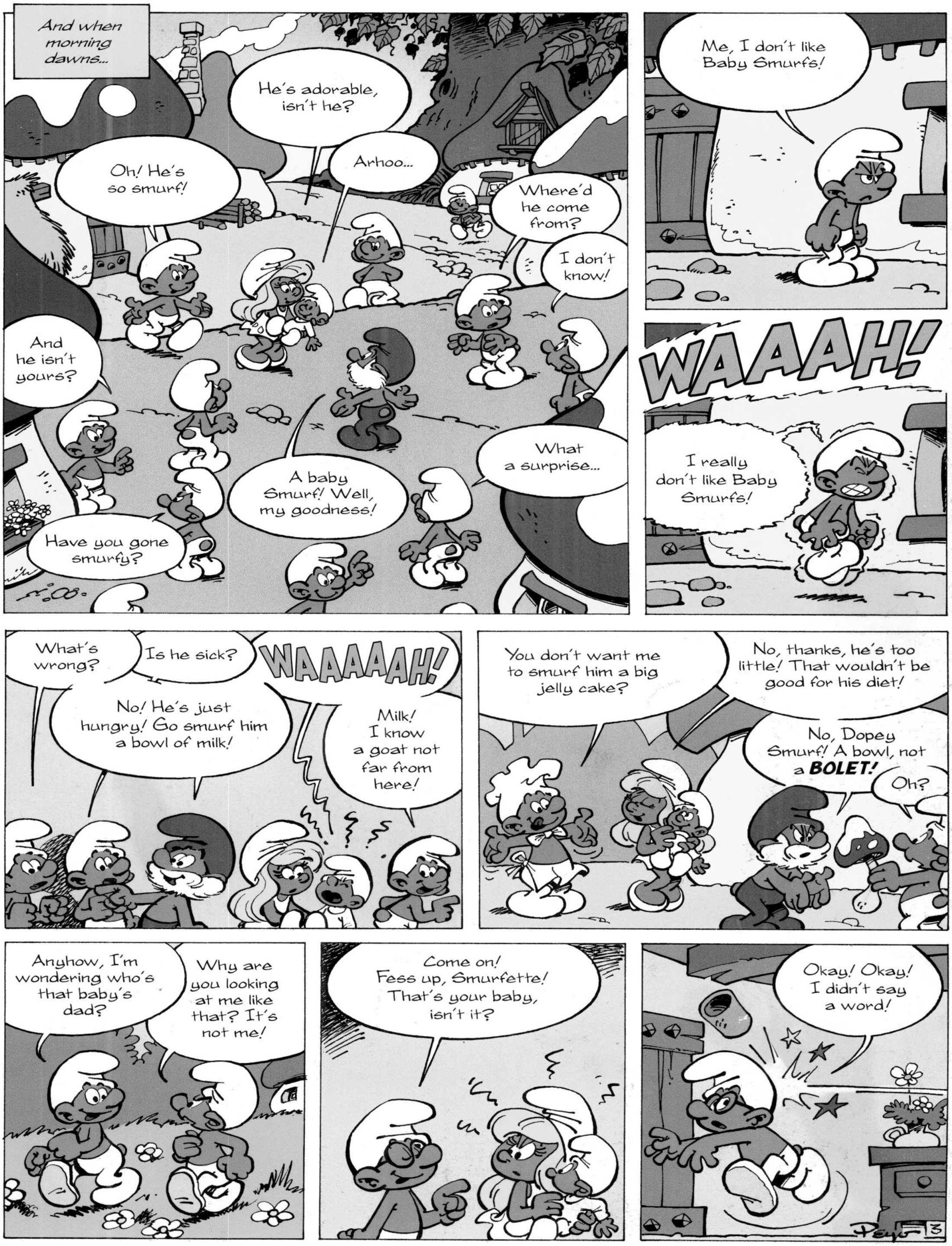

And when morning dawns...
He's adorable, isn't he?
Oh! He's so smurf!
Arhoo...
Where'd he come from?
I don't know!
And he isn't yours?
A baby Smurf! Well, my goodness!
What a surprise...
Have you gone smurfy?
Me, I don't like Baby Smurfs!
WAAAH!
I really don't like Baby Smurfs!
What's wrong?
Is he sick?
WAAAAAH!
No! He's just hungry! Go smurf him a bowl of milk!
Milk! I know a goat not far from here!
You don't want me to smurf him a big jelly cake?
No, thanks, he's too little! That wouldn't be good for his diet!
No, Dopey Smurf! A bowl, not a BOLET!
Oh?
Anyhow, I'm wondering who's that baby's dad?
Why are you looking at me like that? It's not me!
Come on! Fess up, Smurfette! That's your baby, isn't it?
Okay! Okay! I didn't say a word!

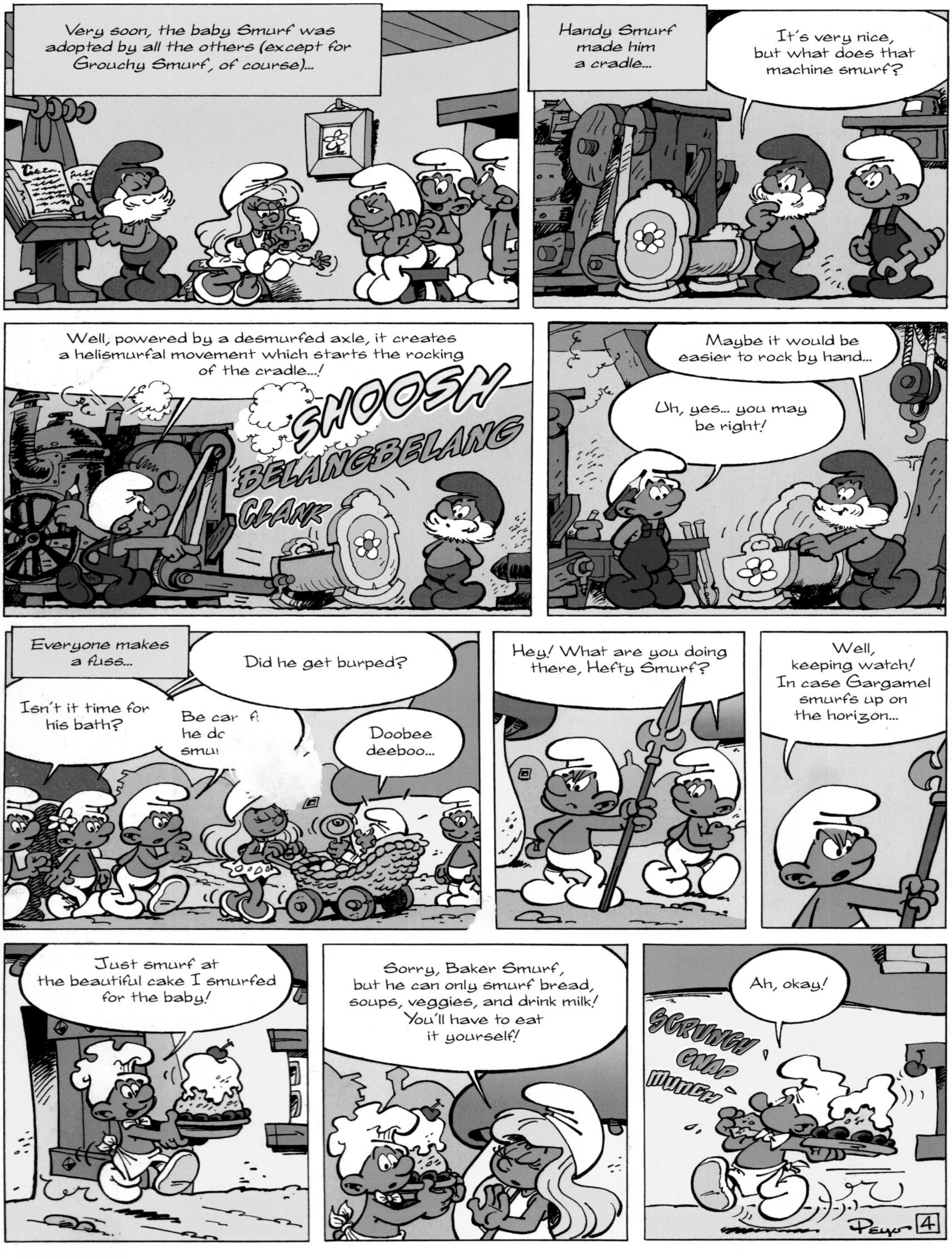
Very soon, the baby Smurf was adopted by all the others (except for Grouchy Smurf, of course)...
Handy Smurf made him a cradle...
It's very nice, but what does that machine smurf?
Well, powered by a desmurfed axle, it creates a helismurfal movement which starts the rocking of the cradle...!
SHOOSH
BELANGBELANG
CLANK
Maybe it would be easier to rock by hand...
Uh, yes... you may be right!
Everyone makes a fuss...
Did he get burped?
Isn't it time for his bath?
Be car
he do
smu
Doobee deeboo...
Hey! What are you doing there, Hefty Smurf?
Well, keeping watch! In case Gargamel smurfs up on the horizon...
Just smurf at the beautiful cake I smurfed for the baby!
Sorry, Baker Smurf, but he can only smurf bread, soups, veggies, and drink milk! You'll have to eat it yourself!
Ah, okay!
SCRUNCH
GNAP
MUNCH
Peyo
4

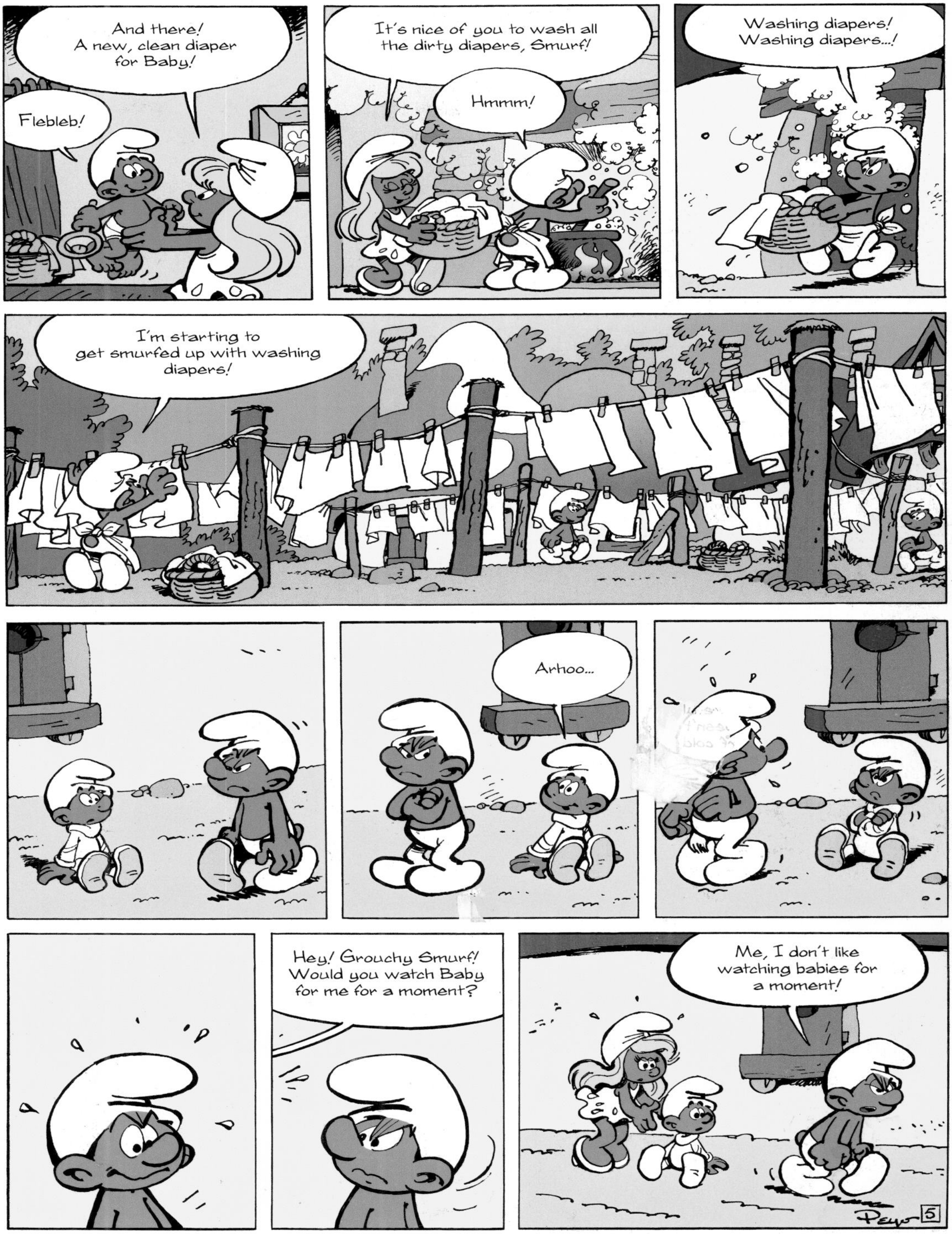

And there! A new, clean diaper for Baby!
Flebleb!
It's nice of you to wash all the dirty diapers, Smurf!
Hmmm!
Washing diapers! Washing diapers...!
I'm starting to get smurfed up with washing diapers!
Arhoo...
Hey! Grouchy Smurf! Would you watch Baby for me for a moment?
Me, I don't like watching babies for a moment!
5

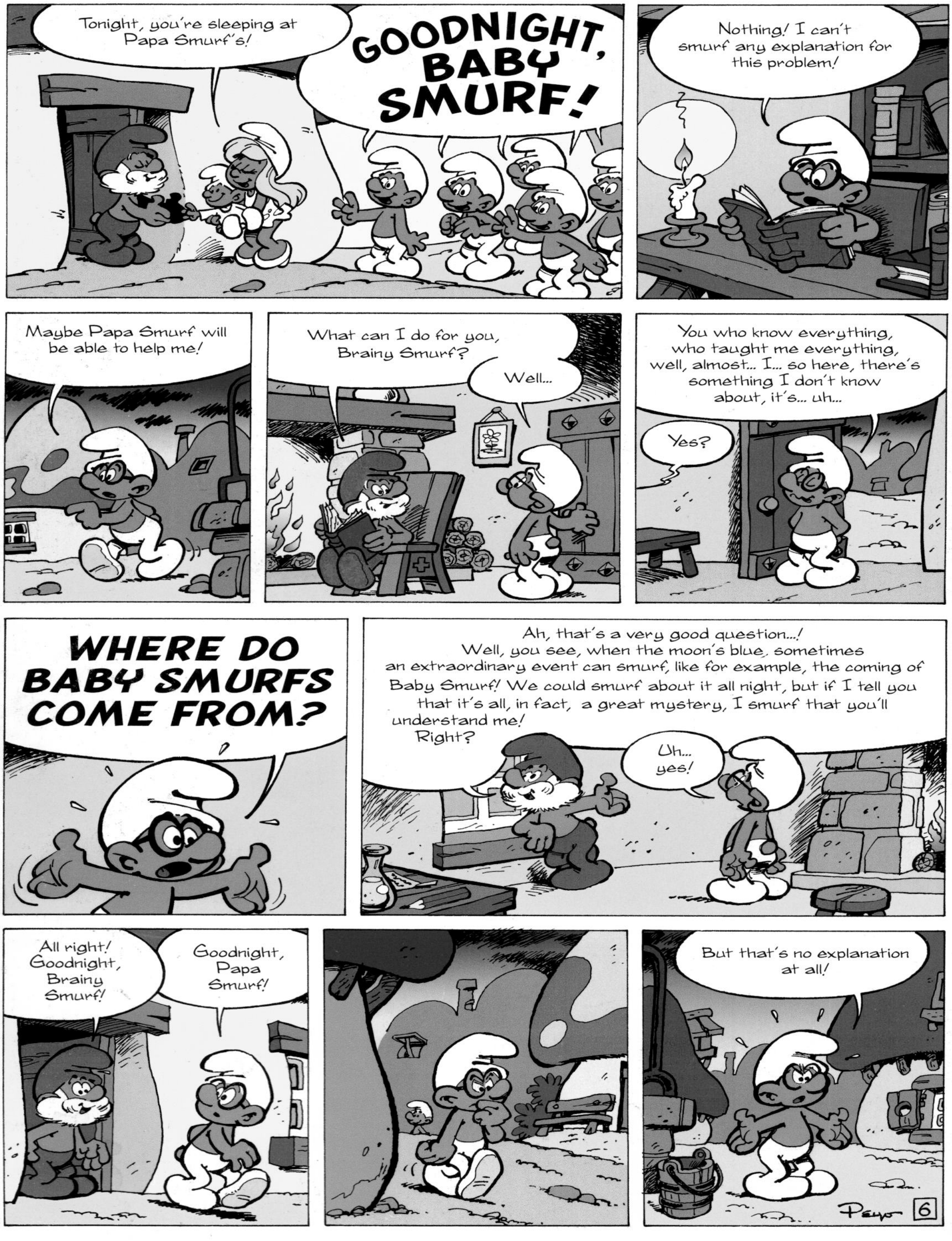
Tonight, you're sleeping at Papa Smurf's!
GOODNIGHT, BABY SMURF!
Nothing! I can't smurf any explanation for this problem!
Maybe Papa Smurf will be able to help me!
What can I do for you, Brainy Smurf?
Well...
You who know everything, who taught me everything, well, almost... I... so here, there's something I don't know about, it's... uh...
Yes?
WHERE DO BABY SMURFS COME FROM?
Ah, that's a very good question...! Well, you see, when the moon's blue, sometimes an extraordinary event can smurf, like for example, the coming of Baby Smurf! We could smurf about it all night, but if I tell you that it's all, in fact, a great mystery, I smurf that you'll understand me! Right?
Uh... yes!
All right! Goodnight, Brainy Smurf!
Goodnight, Papa Smurf!
But that's no explanation at all!
Peyo
6

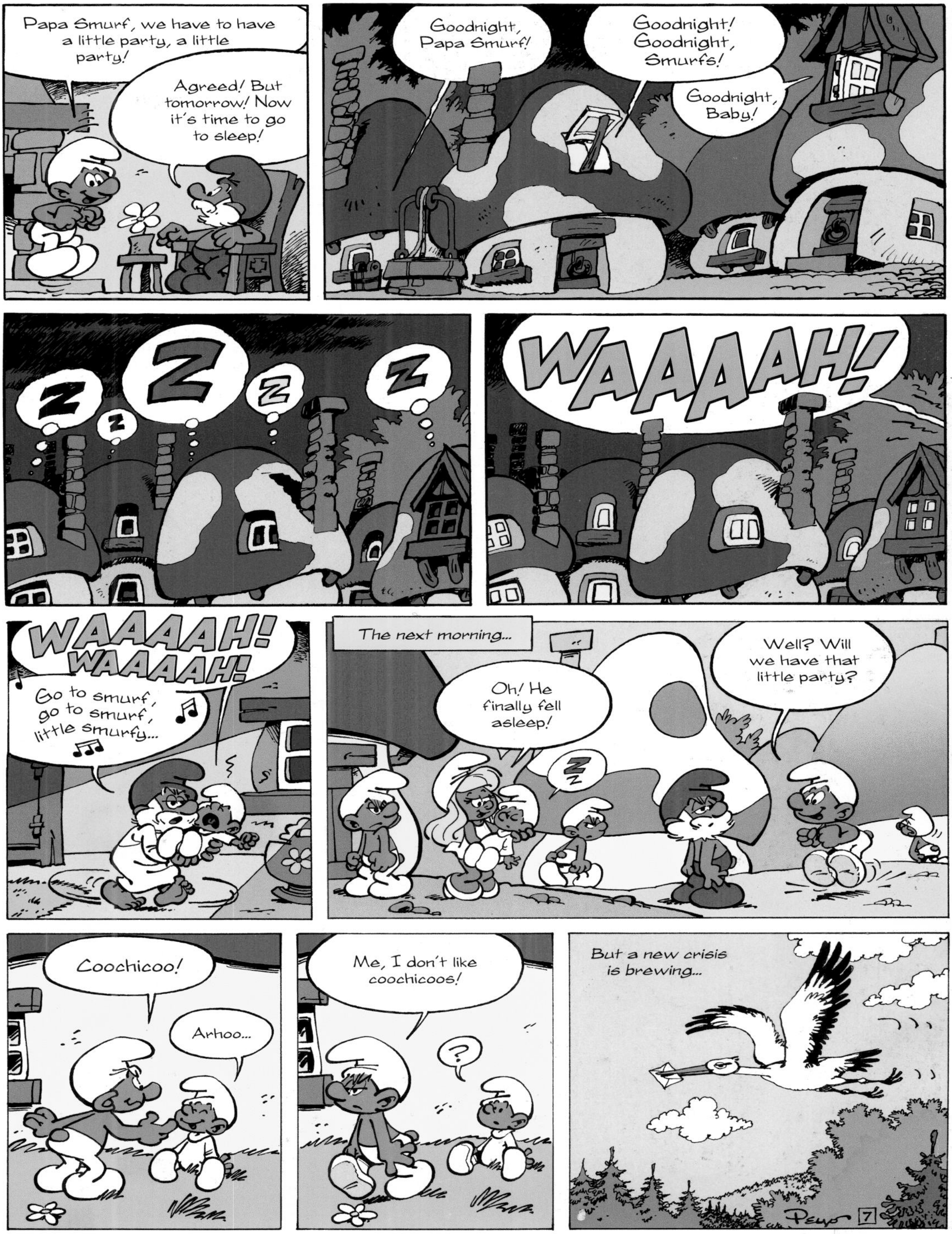
Papa Smurf, we have to have a little party, a little party!
Agreed! But tomorrow! Now it's time to go to sleep!
Goodnight, Papa Smurf!
Goodnight! Goodnight, Smurfs!
Goodnight, Baby!
Z
Z
Z
Z
Z
WAAAAH!
WAAAAH! WAAAAH!
Go to smurf, go to smurf, little smurfy...
The next morning...
Oh! He finally fell asleep!
Z
Well? Will we have that little party?
Coochicoo!
Arhoo...
Me, I don't like coochicoos!
?
But a new crisis is brewing...
Peyo
7

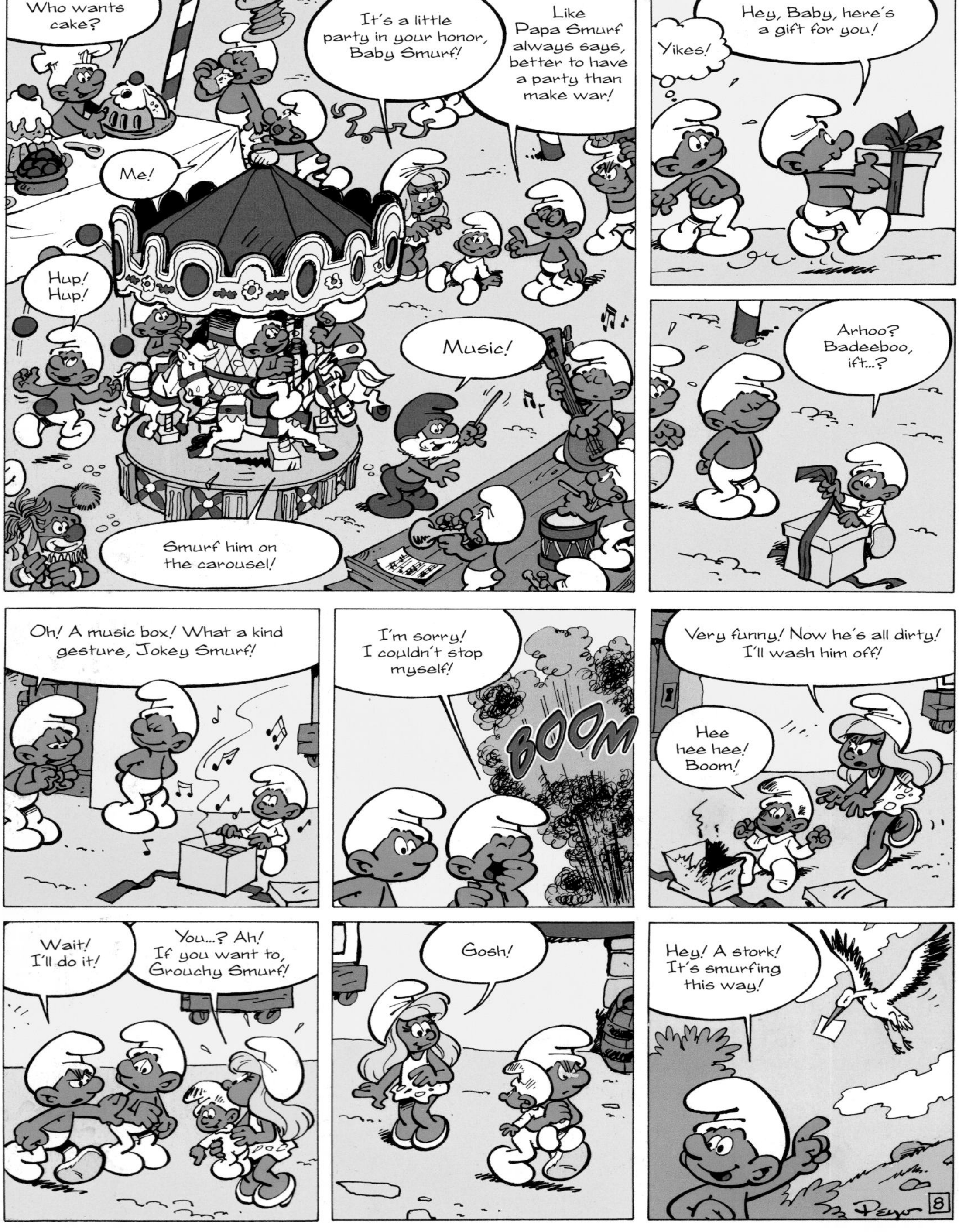

Who wants cake?
It's a little party in your honor, Baby Smurf!
Like Papa Smurf always says, better to have a party than make war!
Me!
Hup! Hup!
Music!
Smurf him on the carousel!
Yikes!
Hey, Baby, here's a gift for you!
Arhoo? Badeeboo, ift...?
Oh! A music box! What a kind gesture, Jokey Smurf!
I'm sorry! I couldn't stop myself!
BOOM
Very funny! Now he's all dirty! I'll wash him off!
Hee hee hee! Boom!
Wait! I'll do it!
You...? Ah! If you want to, Grouchy Smurf!
Gosh!
Hey! A stork! It's smurfing this way!
Peyo
8

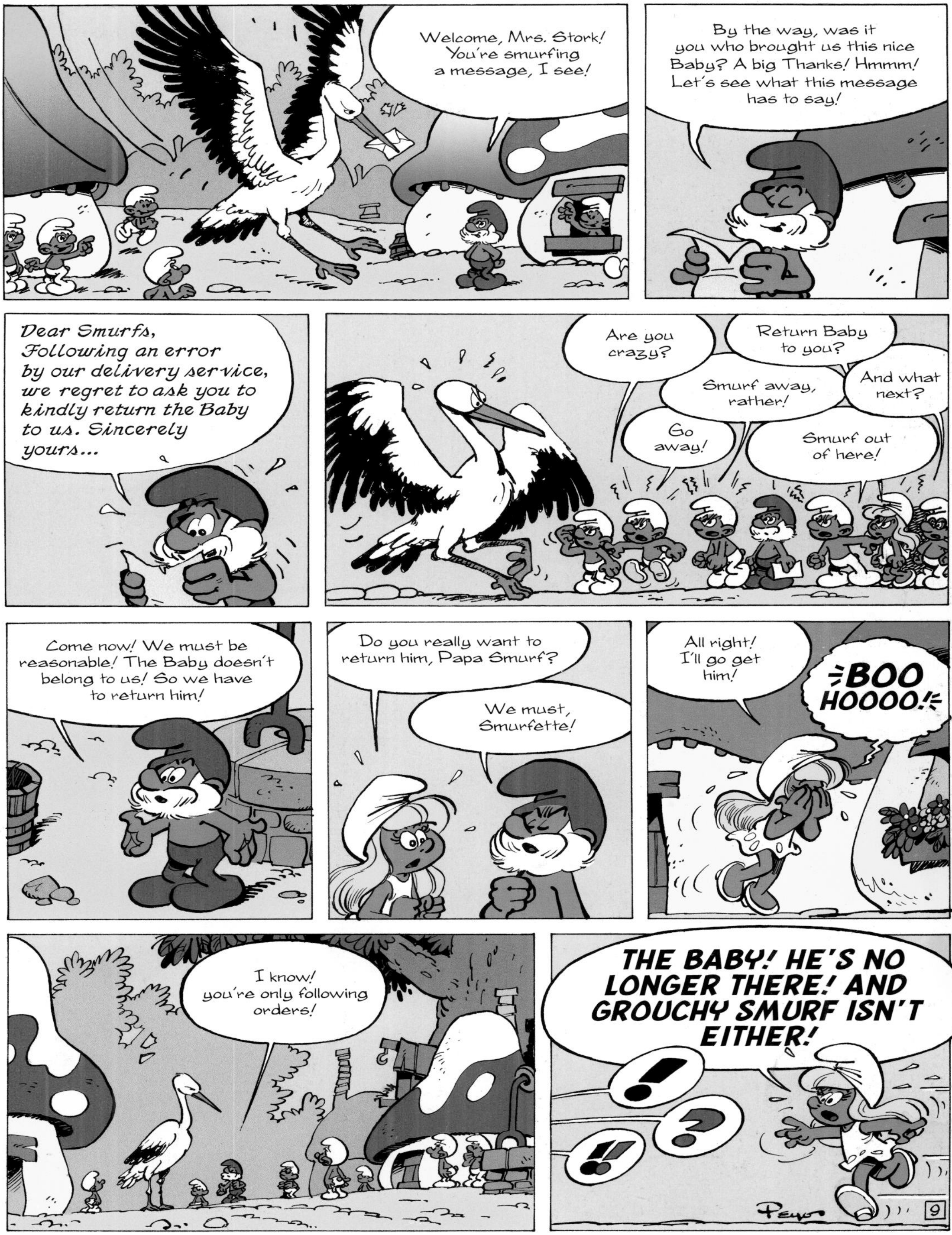
Welcome, Mrs. Stork! You're smurfing a message, I see!
By the way, was it you who brought us this nice Baby? A big Thanks! Hmmm! Let's see what this message has to say!
Dear Smurfs, Following an error by our delivery service, we regret to ask you to kindly return the Baby to us. Sincerely yours...
Are you crazy?
Return Baby to you?
Smurf away, rather!
And what next?
Go away!
Smurf out of here!
Come now! We must be reasonable! The Baby doesn't belong to us! So we have to return him!
Do you really want to return him, Papa Smurf?
We must, Smurfette!
All right! I'll go get him!
BOO HOOOO!
I know! you're only following orders!
THE BABY! HE'S NO LONGER THERE! AND GROUCHY SMURF ISN'T EITHER!
!
?
!!
9

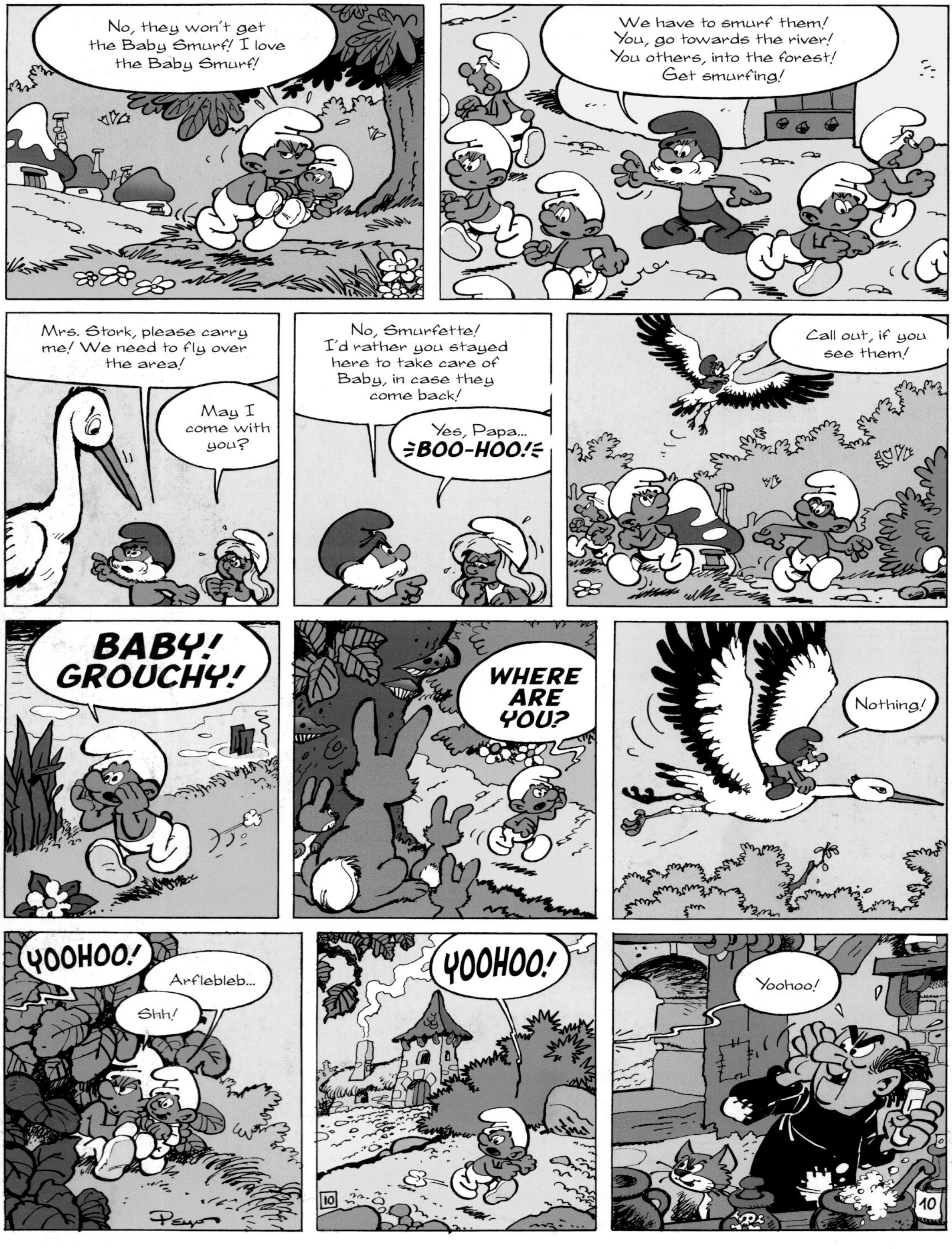
No, they won't get the Baby Smurf! I love the Baby Smurf!
We have to smurf them! You, go towards the river! You others, into the forest! Get smurfing!
Mrs. Stork, please carry me! We need to fly over the area!
May I come with you?
No, Smurfette! I'd rather you stayed here to take care of Baby, in case they come back!
Yes, Papa... BOO-HOO!
Call out, if you see them!
BABY! GROUCHY!
WHERE ARE YOU?
Nothing!
YOOHOO!
Arflebleb...
Shh!
YOOHOO!
Yoohoo!

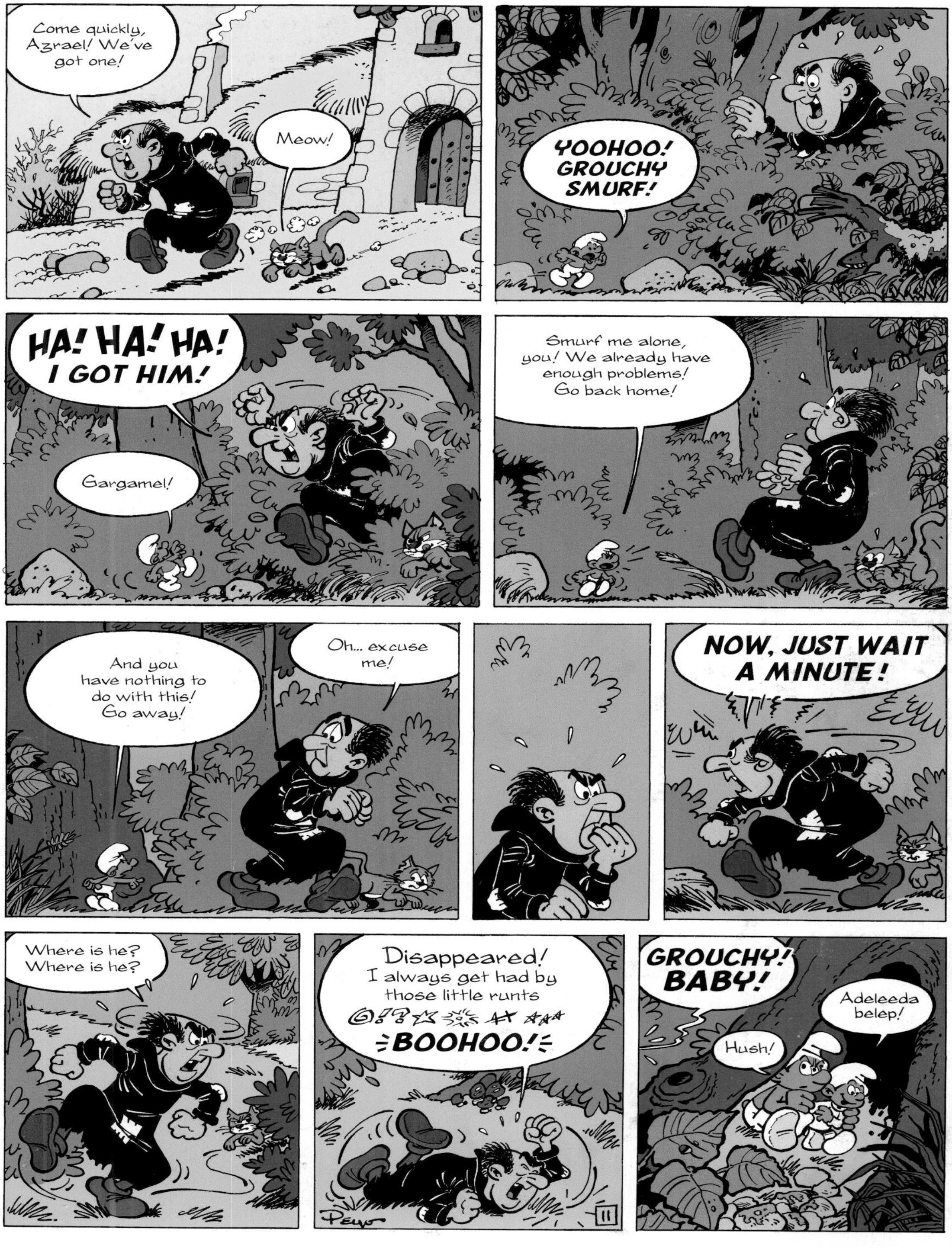
Come quickly, Azrael! We've got one!
Meow!
YOOHOO! GROUCHY SMURF!
HA! HA! HA! I GOT HIM!
Gargamel!
Smurf me alone, you! We already have enough problems! Go back home!
And you have nothing to do with this! Go away!
Oh... excuse me!
NOW, JUST WAIT A MINUTE!
Where is he? Where is he?
Disappeared! I always get had by those little runts
BOOHOO!
GROUCHY! BABY!
Hush!
Adeleeda belep!

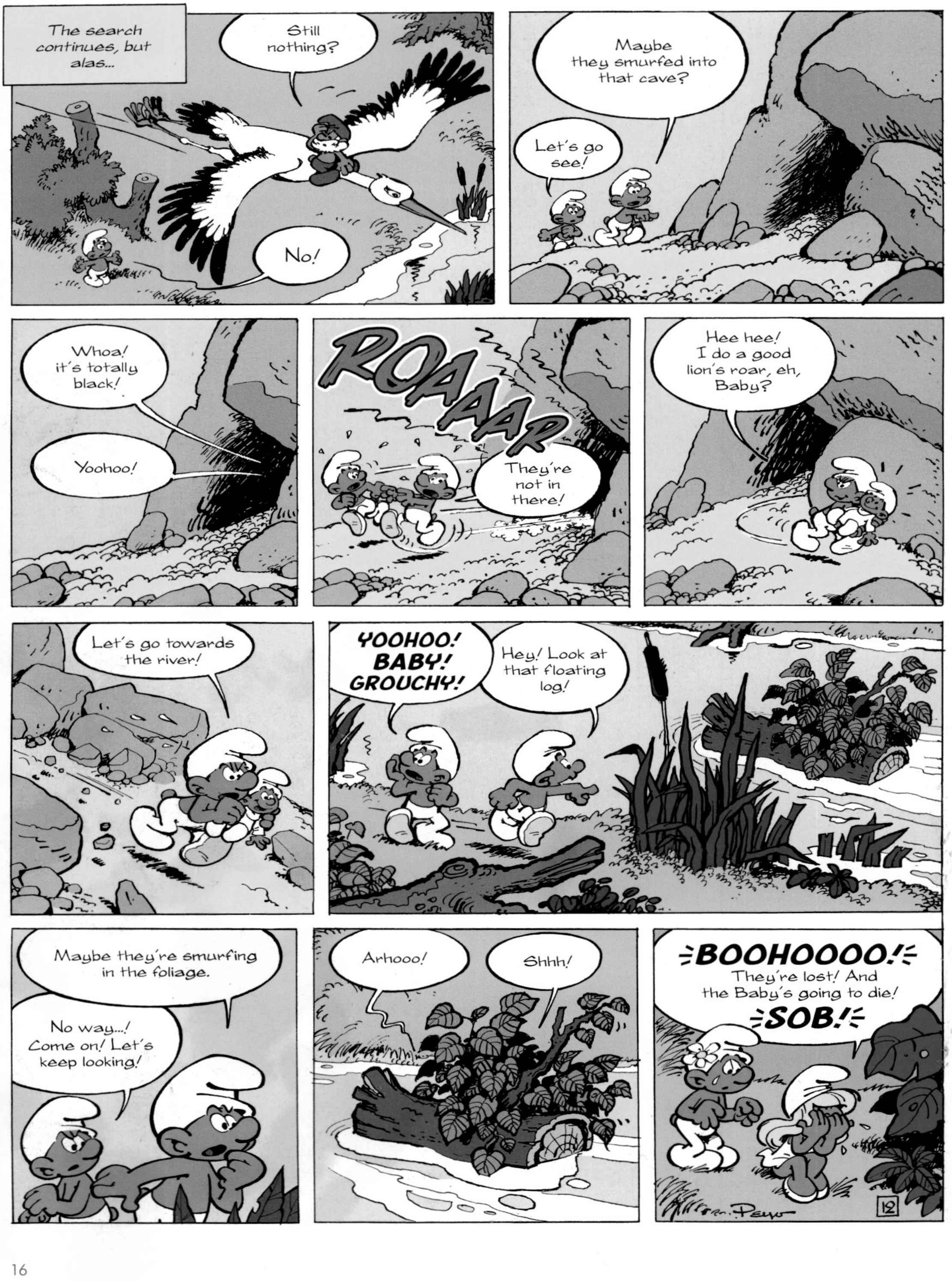
The search continues, but alas...
Still nothing?
No!
Maybe they smurfed into that cave?
Let's go see!
Whoa! it's totally black!
Yoohoo!
ROAAAAR
They're not in there!
Hee hee! I do a good lion's roar, eh, Baby?
Let's go towards the river!
YOOHOO! BABY! GROUCHY!
Hey! Look at that floating log!
Maybe they're smurfing in the foliage.
No way...! Come on! Let's keep looking!
Arhooo!
Shhh!
BOOHOOOO! They're lost! And the Baby's going to die! SOB!
12

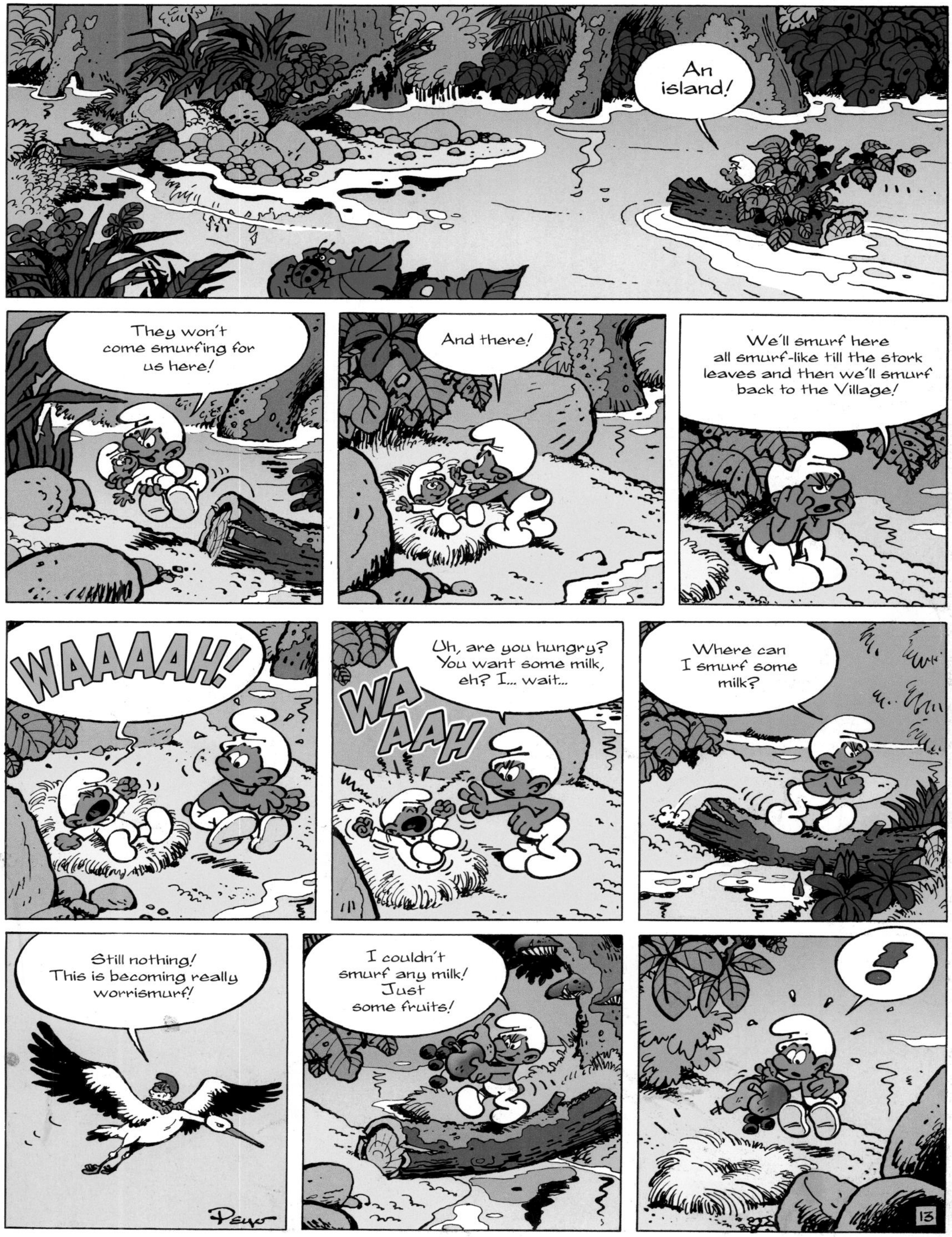

An island!
They won't come smurfing for us here!
And there!
We'll smurf here all smurf-like till the stork leaves and then we'll smurf back to the Village!
WAAAAAH!
WA AAH
Uh, are you hungry? You want some milk, eh? I... wait...
Where can I smurf some milk?
Still nothing! This is becoming really worrismurf!
Peyo
I couldn't smurf any milk! Just some fruits!
!
13

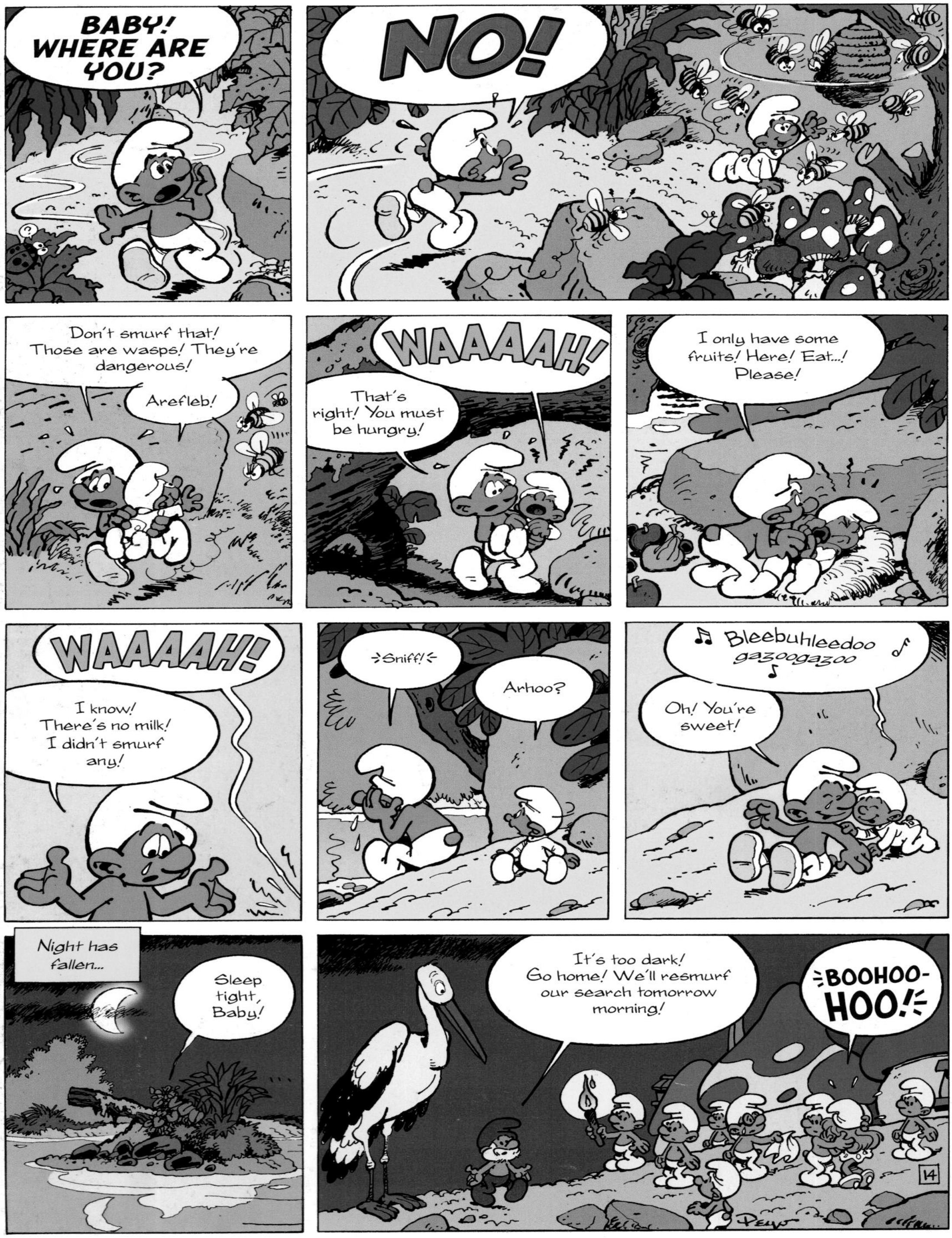
BABY! WHERE ARE YOU?
NO!
Don't smurf that! Those are wasps! They're dangerous!
Arefleb!
WAAAAH!
That's right! You must be hungry!
I only have some fruits! Here! Eat...! Please!
WAAAAH!
I know! There's no milk! I didn't smurf any!
Sniff!
Arhoo?
Bleebuhleedoo gazoogazoo
Oh! You're sweet!
Night has fallen...
Sleep tight, Baby!
It's too dark! Go home! We'll resmurf our search tomorrow morning!
BOOHOO-HOO!
14

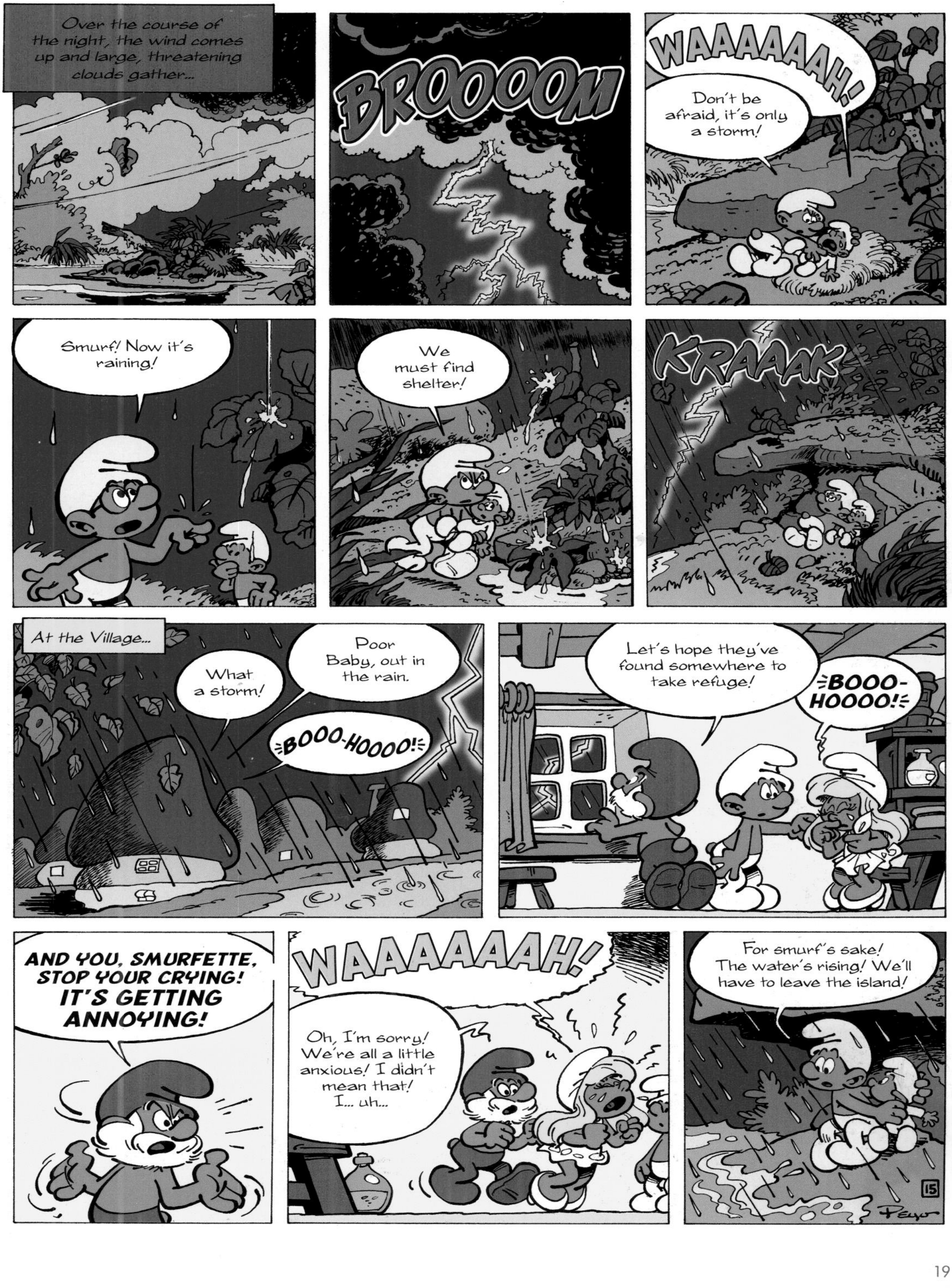

Over the course of the night, the wind comes up and large, threatening clouds gather...
BROOOOM
WAAAAAAAH!
Don't be afraid, it's only a storm!
Smurf! Now it's raining!
We must find shelter!
KRAAAK
At the Village...
What a storm!
Poor Baby, out in the rain.
BOOO-HOOOO!
Let's hope they've found somewhere to take refuge!
BOOO-HOOOO!
AND YOU, SMURFETTE, STOP YOUR CRYING! IT'S GETTING ANNOYING!
WAAAAAAAH!
Oh, I'm sorry! We're all a little anxious! I didn't mean that! I... uh...
For smurf's sake! The water's rising! We'll have to leave the island!
15

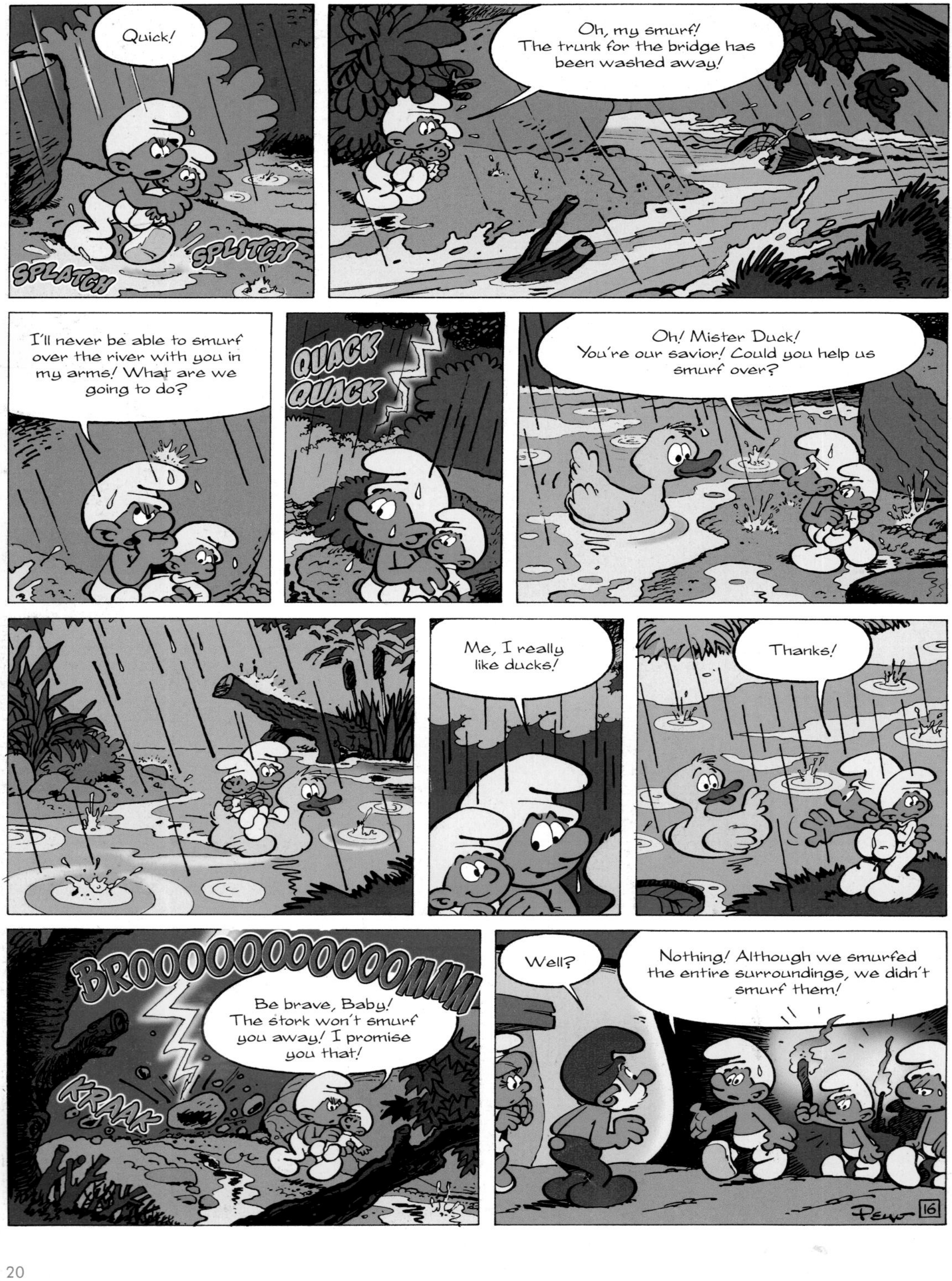
Quick!
SPLATCH
SPLITCH
Oh, my smurf! The trunk for the bridge has been washed away!
I'll never be able to smurf over the river with you in my arms! What are we going to do?
QUACK QUACK
Oh! Mister Duck! You're our savior! Could you help us smurf over?
Me, I really like ducks!
Thanks!
BROOOOOOOOOOOMMM
Be brave, Baby! The stork won't smurf you away! I promise you that!
KRAAK
Well?
Nothing! Although we smurfed the entire surroundings, we didn't smurf them!
Peyo
16

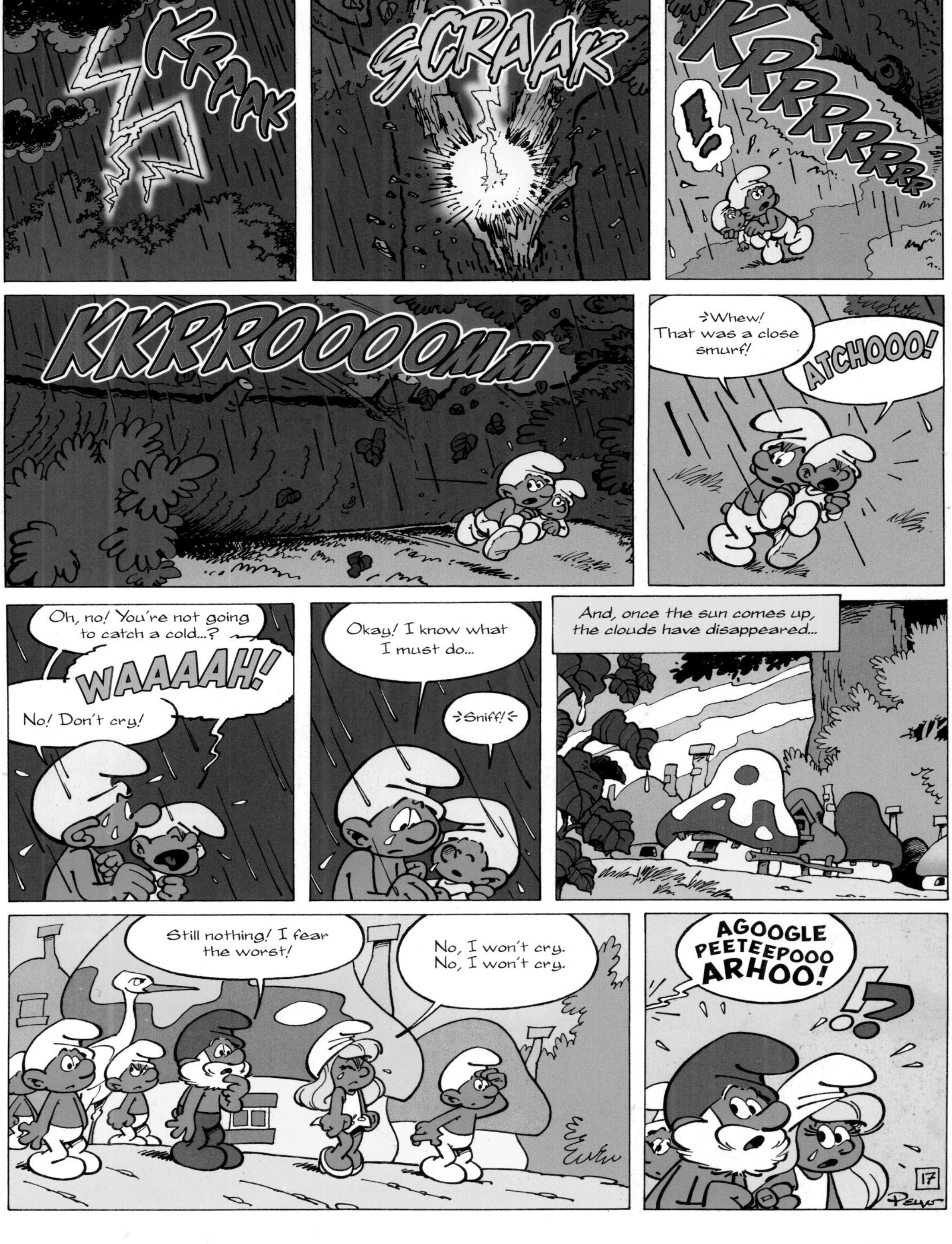

KRAAK
SCRAAK
KRRRRRRRR
!
KKRROOOOOMM
Whew! That was a close smurf!
ATCHOOO!
Oh, no! You're not going to catch a cold...?
WAAAAH!
No! Don't cry!
Okay! I know what I must do...
Sniff!
And, once the sun comes up, the clouds have disappeared...
Still nothing! I fear the worst!
No, I won't cry. No, I won't cry.
AGOOGLE PEETEEPOOO ARHOO!
!??
17

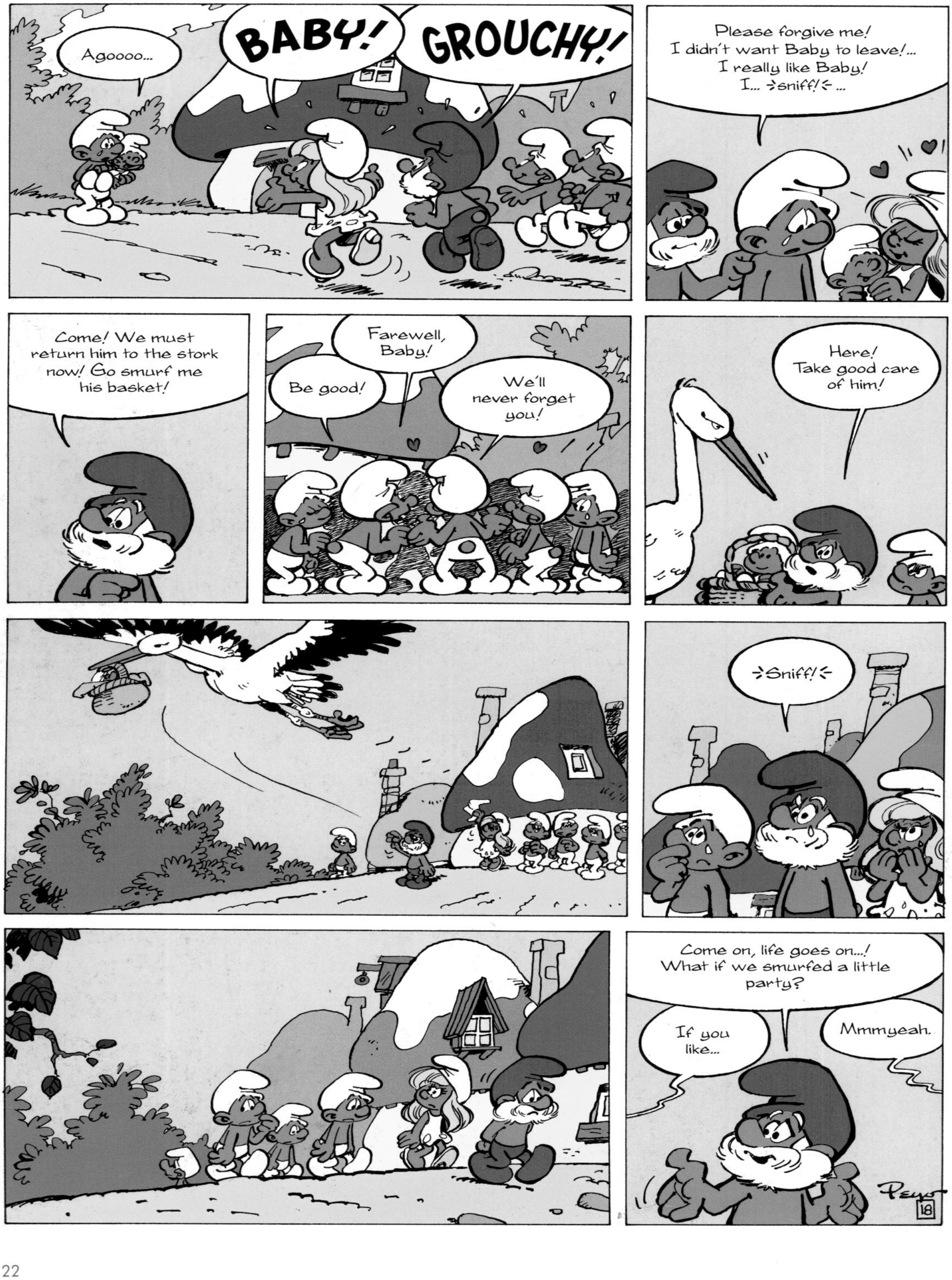

Agoooo...
BABY!
GROUCHY!
Please forgive me!
I didn't want Baby to leave!...
I really like Baby!
I... ⋟sniff!⋞ ...
Come! We must return him to the stork now! Go smurf me his basket!
Farewell, Baby!
Be good!
We'll never forget you!
Here! Take good care of him!
⋟Sniff!⋞
Come on, life goes on...! What if we smurfed a little party?
If you like...
Mmmyeah.
Peyo
18

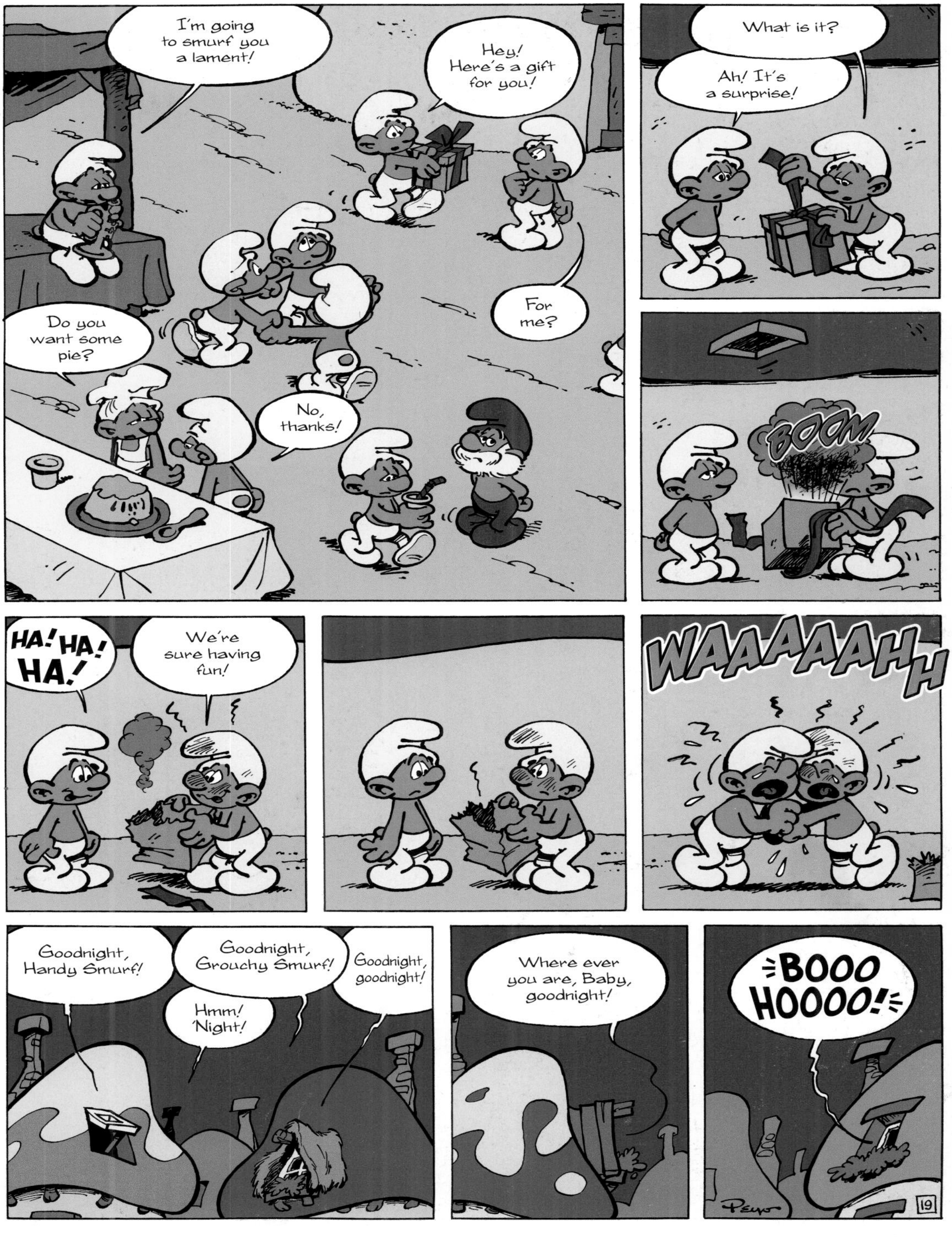
I'm going to smurf you a lament!
Hey! Here's a gift for you!
For me?
Do you want some pie?
No, thanks!
What is it?
Ah! It's a surprise!
BOOM
HA! HA! HA!
We're sure having fun!
WAAAAAHH
Goodnight, Handy Smurf!
Goodnight, Grouchy Smurf!
Hmm! 'Night!
Goodnight, goodnight!
Where ever you are, Baby, goodnight!
BOOO HOOOO!
19

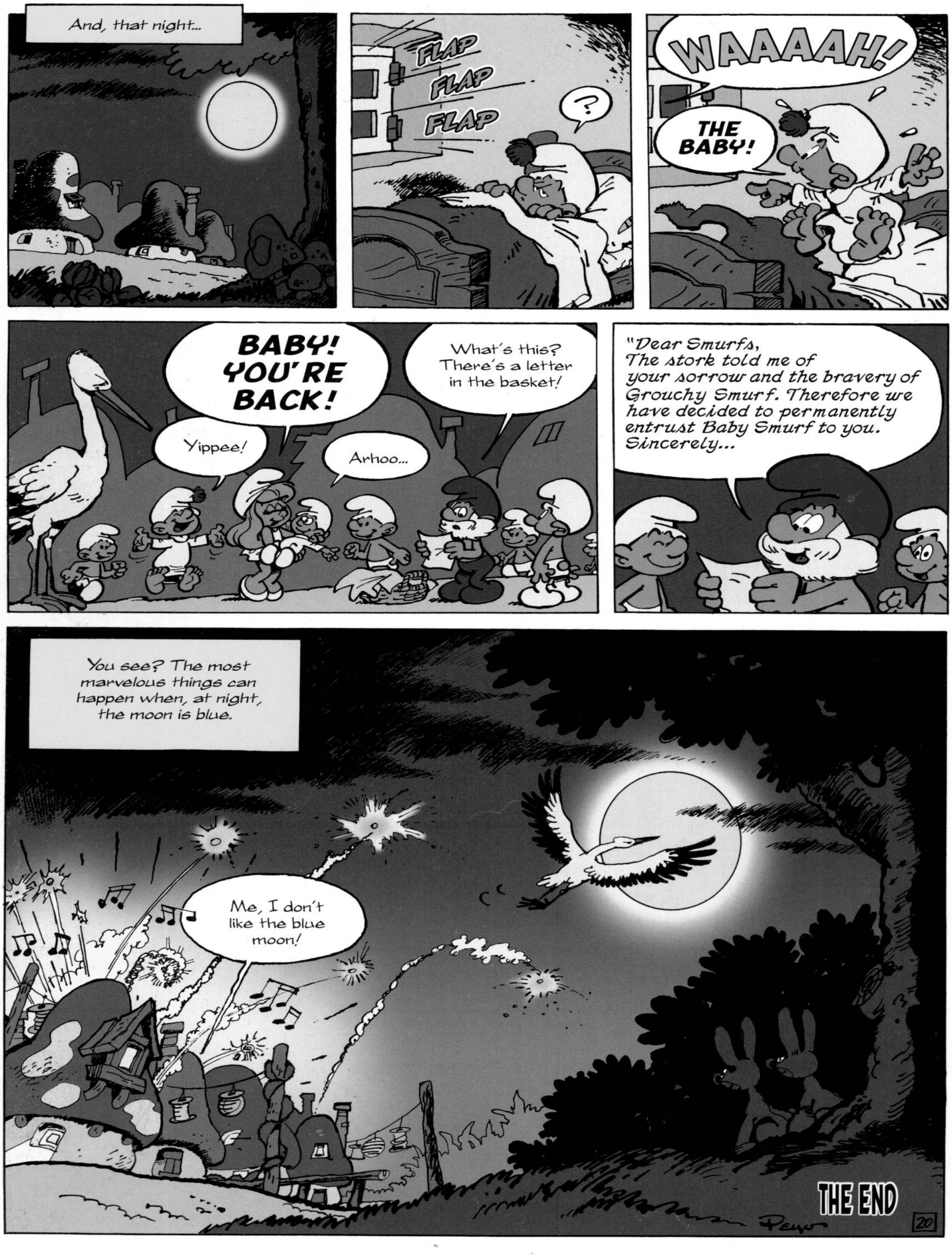

And, that night...
FLAP
FLAP
FLAP
?
WAAAAH!
THE BABY!
BABY! YOU'RE BACK!
Yippee!
Arhoo...
What's this? There's a letter in the basket!
"Dear Smurfs, The stork told me of your sorrow and the bravery of Grouchy Smurf. Therefore we have decided to permanently entrust Baby Smurf to you. Sincerely...
You see? The most marvelous things can happen when, at night, the moon is blue.
Me, I don't like the blue moon!
THE END
Peyo
20

A SMURFING PARTY

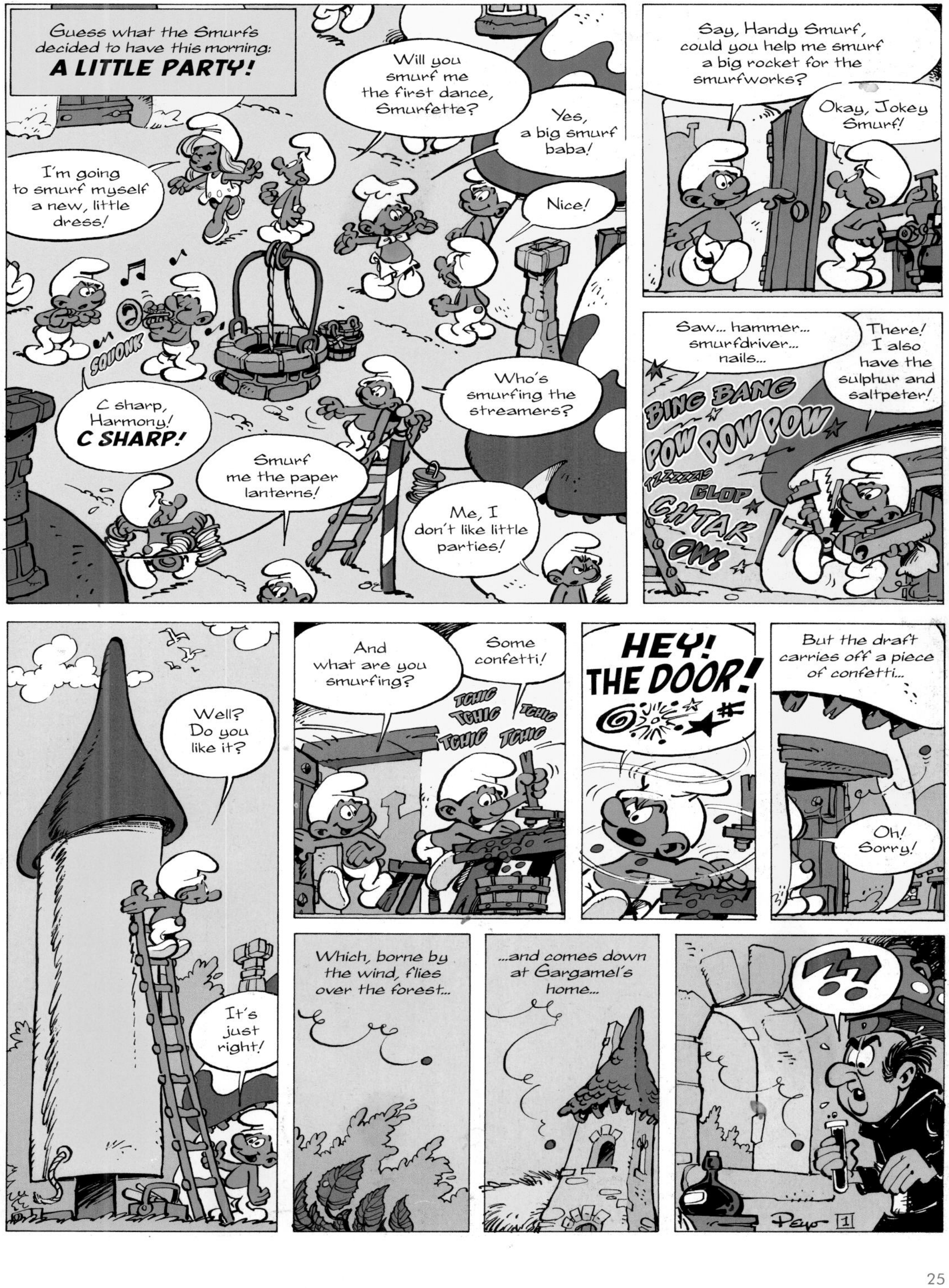

Guess what the Smurfs decided to have this morning: **A LITTLE PARTY!**
Will you smurf me the first dance, Smurfette?
Yes, a big smurf baba!
I'm going to smurf myself a new, little dress!
Nice!
SQUONK
C sharp, Harmony! **C SHARP!**
Who's smurfing the streamers?
Smurf me the paper lanterns!
Me, I don't like little parties!
Say, Handy Smurf, could you help me smurf a big rocket for the smurfworks?
Okay, Jokey Smurf!
Saw... hammer... smurfdriver... nails...
There! I also have the sulphur and saltpeter!
BING BANG
POW POW POW
TZZZZZIS
CLOP
CHTAK
OW!
Well? Do you like it?
It's just right!
And what are you smurfing?
Some confetti!
TCHIC TCHIC TCHIC TCHIC TCHIC
HEY! THE DOOR!
But the draft carries off a piece of confetti...
Oh! Sorry!
Which, borne by the wind, flies over the forest...
...and comes down at Gargamel's home...
Peyo
1

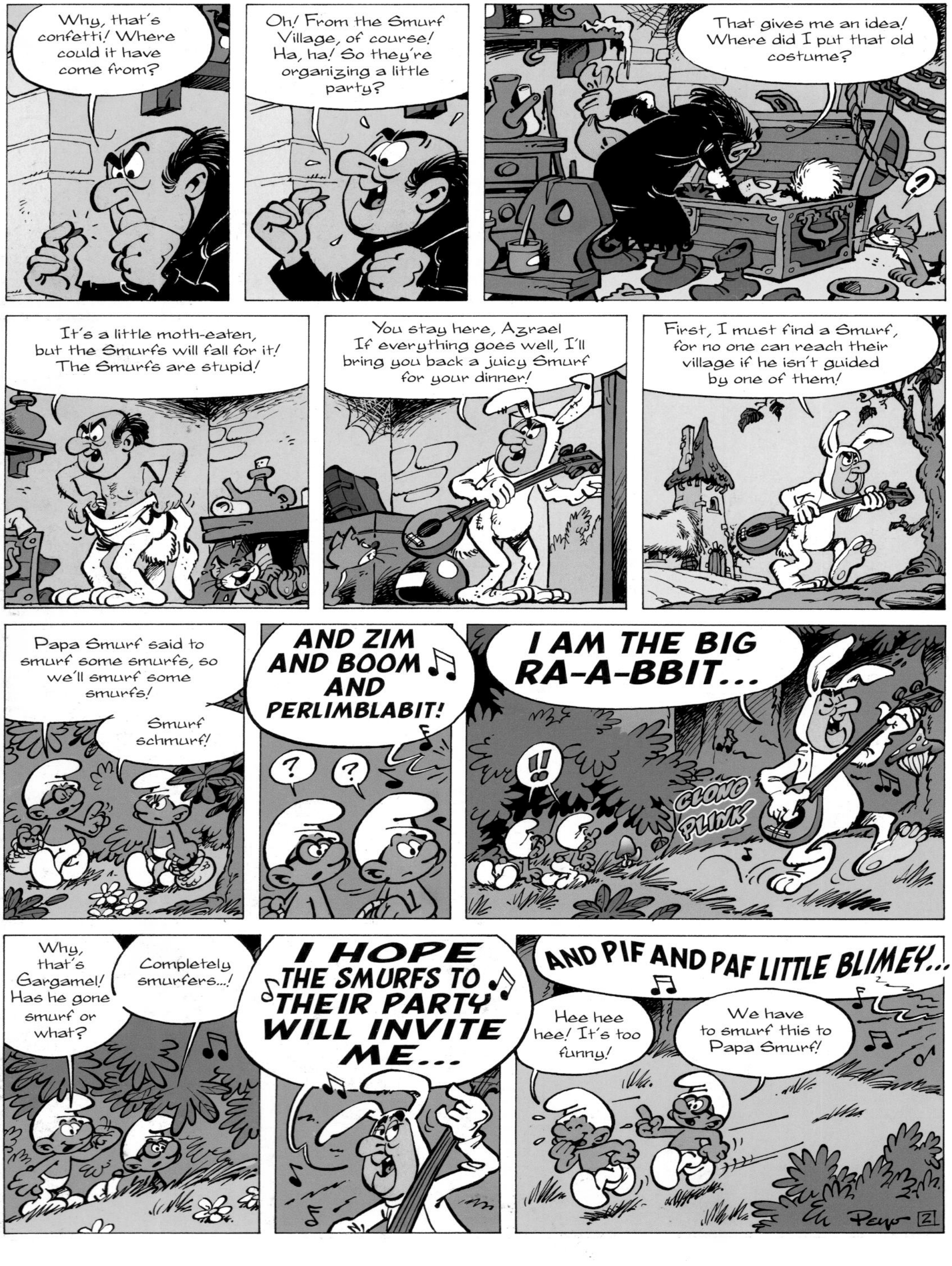

Why, that's confetti! Where could it have come from?
Oh! From the Smurf Village, of course! Ha, ha! So they're organizing a little party?
That gives me an idea! Where did I put that old costume?
It's a little moth-eaten, but the Smurfs will fall for it! The Smurfs are stupid!
You stay here, Azrael If everything goes well, I'll bring you back a juicy Smurf for your dinner!
First, I must find a Smurf, for no one can reach their village if he isn't guided by one of them!
Papa Smurf said to smurf some smurfs, so we'll smurf some smurfs!
Smurf schmurf!
AND ZIM AND BOOM AND PERLIMBLABIT!
?
?
I AM THE BIG RA-A-BBIT...
!!
CLONG
PLINK
Why, that's Gargamel! Has he gone smurf or what?
Completely smurfers...!
I HOPE THE SMURFS TO THEIR PARTY WILL INVITE ME...
AND PIF AND PAF LITTLE BLIMEY...
Hee hee hee! It's too funny!
We have to smurf this to Papa Smurf!
Peyo
2

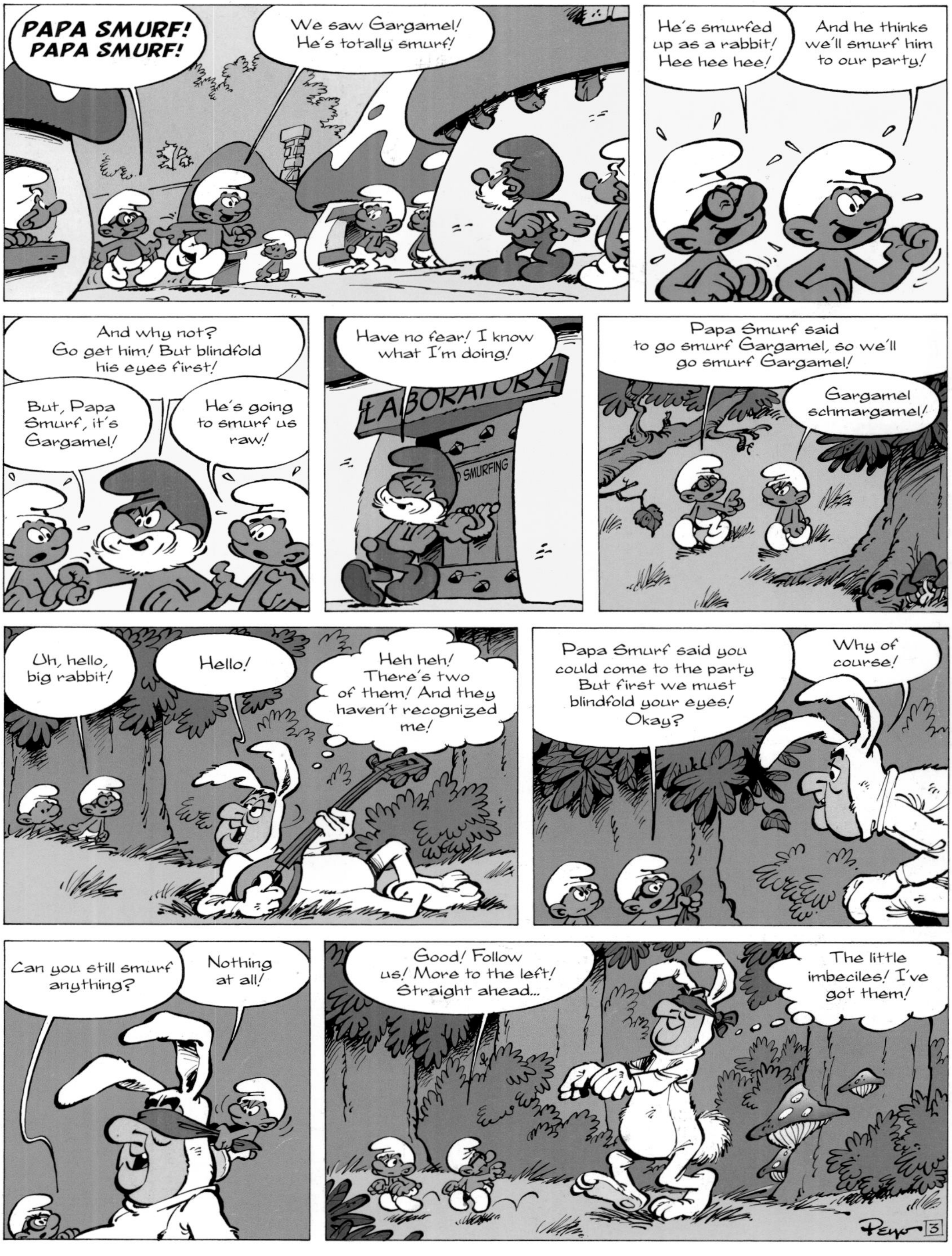

PAPA SMURF! PAPA SMURF!
We saw Gargamel! He's totally smurf!
He's smurfed up as a rabbit! Hee hee hee!
And he thinks we'll smurf him to our party!
And why not? Go get him! But blindfold his eyes first!
But, Papa Smurf, it's Gargamel!
He's going to smurf us raw!
Have no fear! I know what I'm doing!
LABORATORY
SMURFING
Papa Smurf said to go smurf Gargamel, so we'll go smurf Gargamel!
Gargamel schmargamel!
Uh, hello, big rabbit!
Hello!
Heh heh! There's two of them! And they haven't recognized me!
Papa Smurf said you could come to the party But first we must blindfold your eyes! Okay?
Why of course!
Can you still smurf anything?
Nothing at all!
Good! Follow us! More to the left! Straight ahead...
The little imbeciles! I've got them!
Peyo 3

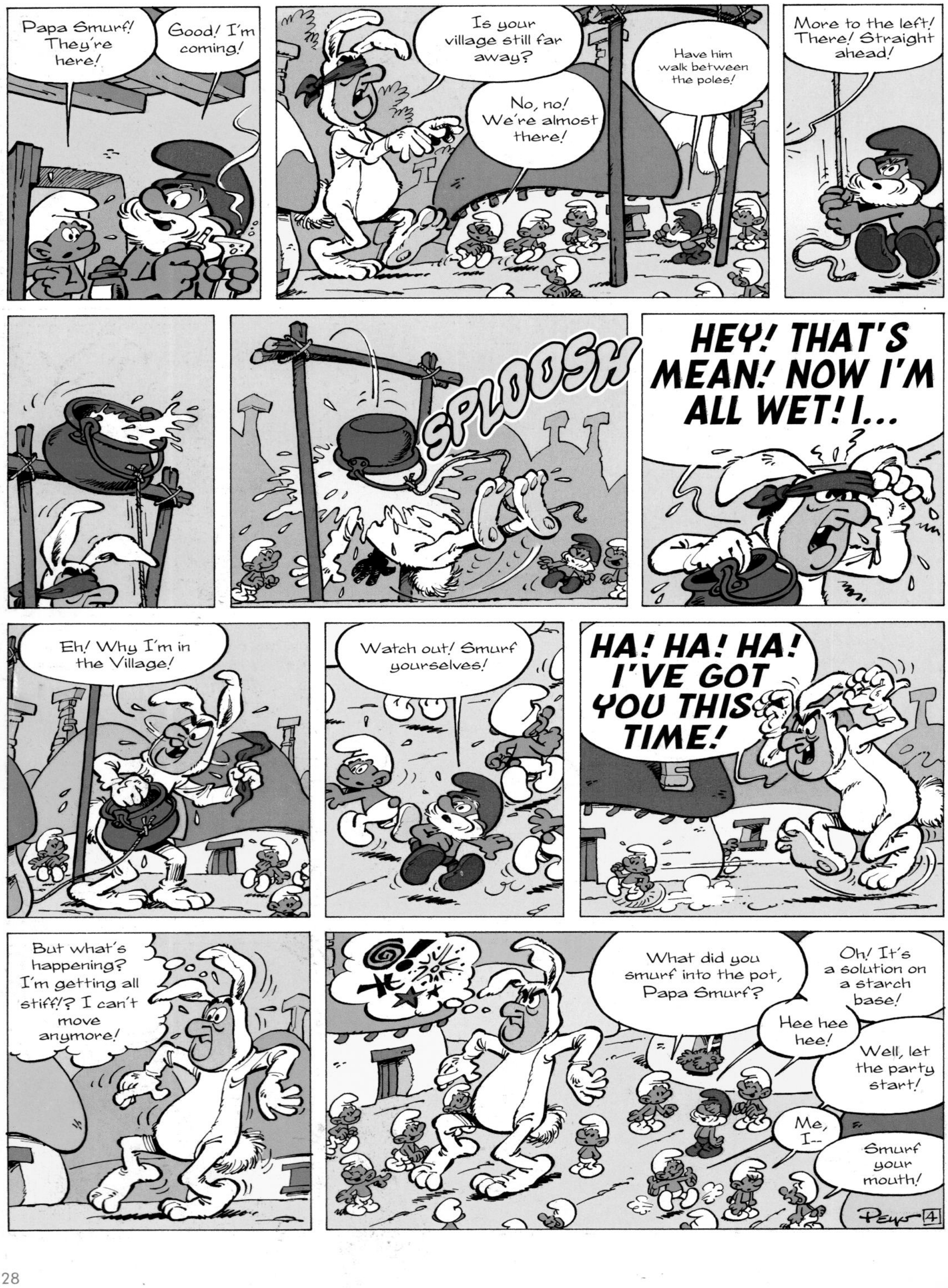

Papa Smurf! They're here!
Good! I'm coming!
Is your village still far away?
No, no! We're almost there!
Have him walk between the poles!
More to the left! There! Straight ahead!
SPLOOSH
HEY! THAT'S MEAN! NOW I'M ALL WET! I...
Eh! Why I'm in the Village!
Watch out! Smurf yourselves!
HA! HA! HA! I'VE GOT YOU THIS TIME!
But what's happening? I'm getting all stiff!? I can't move anymore!
What did you smurf into the pot, Papa Smurf?
Oh! It's a solution on a starch base!
Hee hee hee!
Well, let the party start!
Me, I--
Smurf your mouth!
4

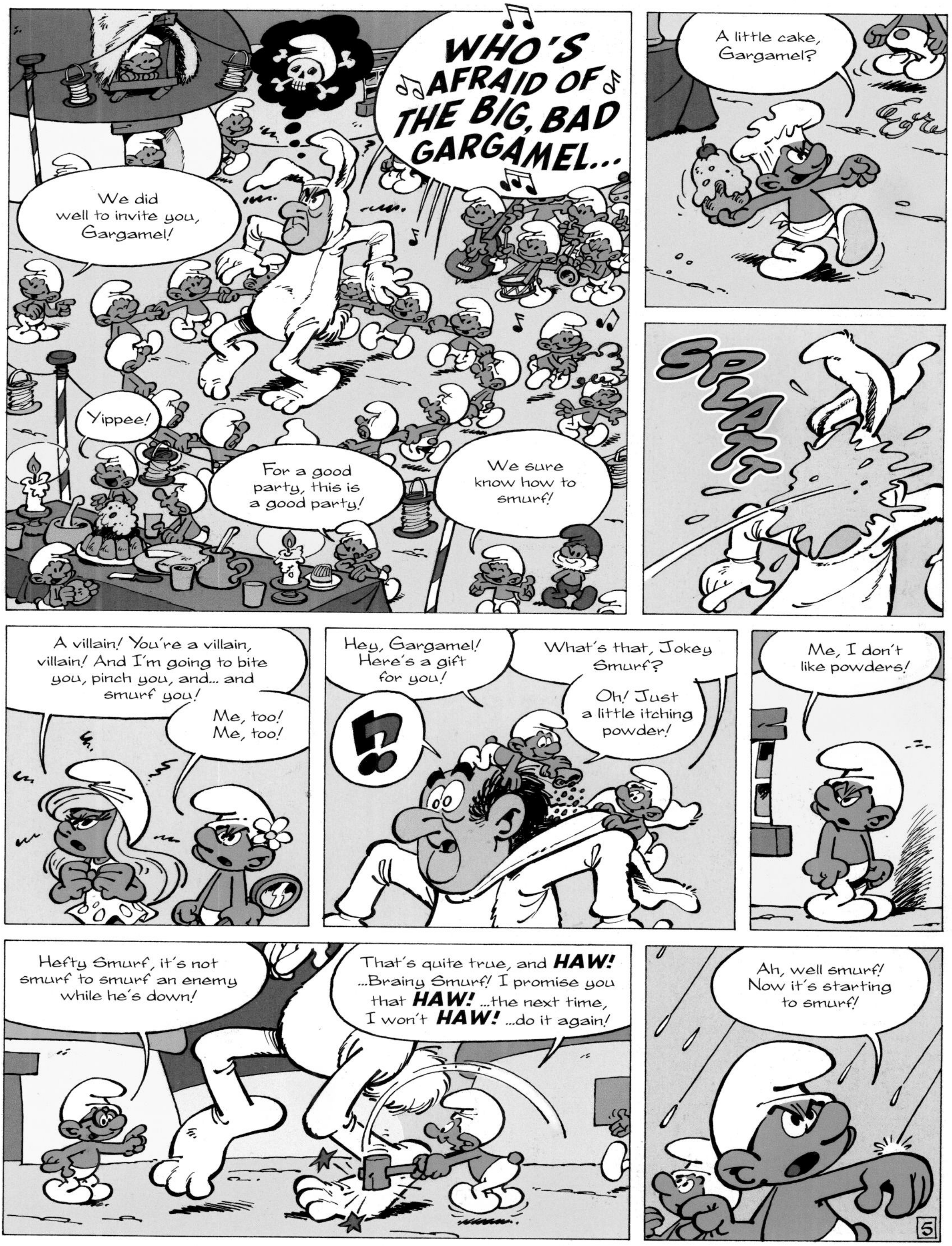

WHO'S AFRAID OF THE BIG, BAD GARGAMEL...
We did well to invite you, Gargamel!
Yippee!
For a good party, this is a good party!
We sure know how to smurf!
A little cake, Gargamel?
SPLATT
A villain! You're a villain, villain! And I'm going to bite you, pinch you, and... and smurf you!
Me, too! Me, too!
Hey, Gargamel! Here's a gift for you!
What's that, Jokey Smurf?
Oh! Just a little itching powder!
Me, I don't like powders!
Hefty Smurf, it's not smurf to smurf an enemy while he's down!
That's quite true, and HAW! ...Brainy Smurf! I promise you that HAW! ...the next time, I won't HAW! ...do it again!
Ah, well smurf! Now it's starting to smurf!
5

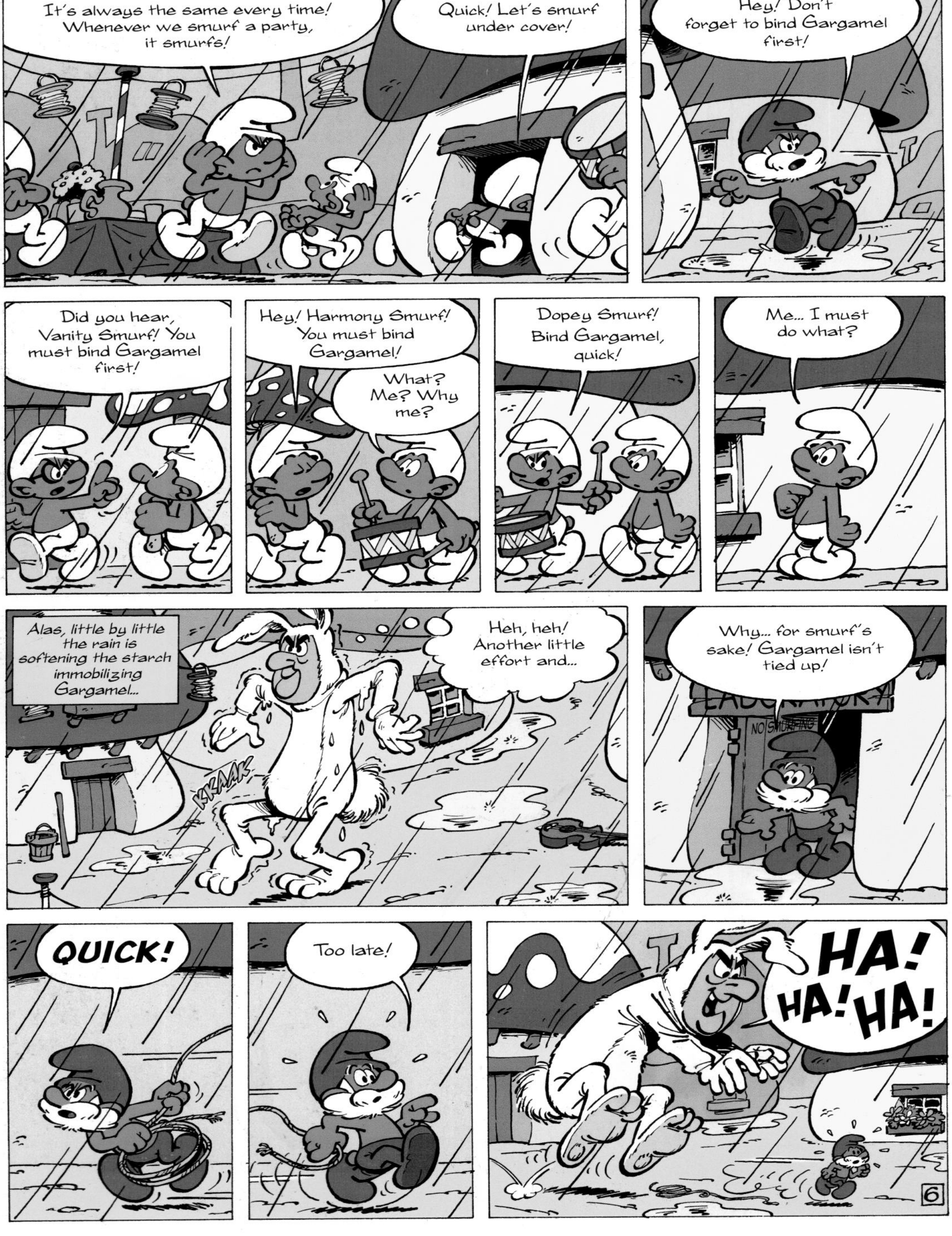

It's always the same every time! Whenever we smurf a party, it smurfs!
Quick! Let's smurf under cover!
Hey! Don't forget to bind Gargamel first!
Did you hear, Vanity Smurf! You must bind Gargamel first!
Hey! Harmony Smurf! You must bind Gargamel!
What? Me? Why me?
Dopey Smurf! Bind Gargamel, quick!
Me... I must do what?
Alas, little by little the rain is softening the starch immobilizing Gargamel...
KRAAK
Heh, heh! Another little effort and...
Why... for smurf's sake! Gargamel isn't tied up!
NO SMURFING
QUICK!
Too late!
HA! HA! HA!
6

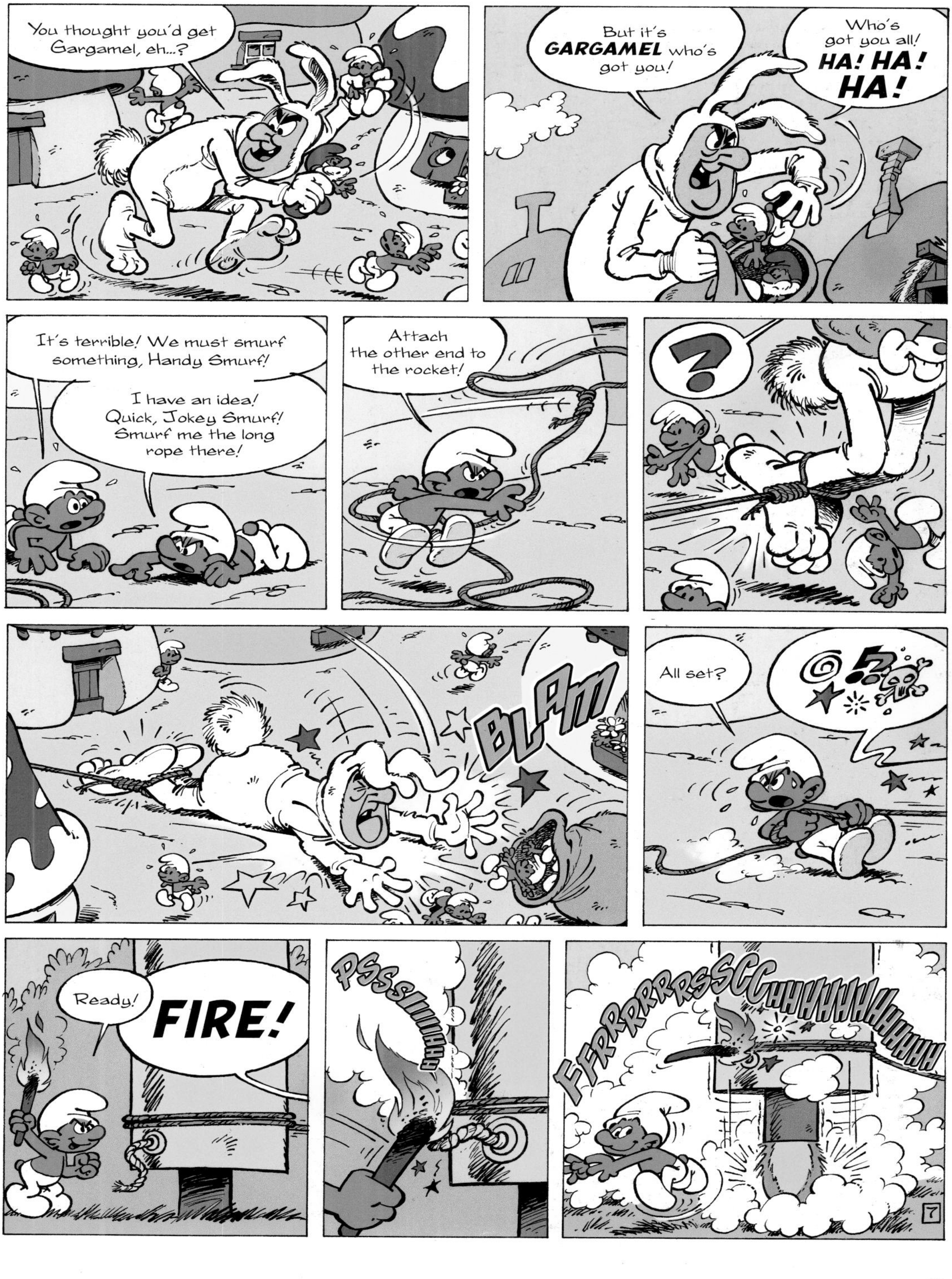
You thought you'd get Gargamel, eh...?
But it's GARGAMEL who's got you!
Who's got you all! HA! HA! HA!
It's terrible! We must smurf something, Handy Smurf!
I have an idea! Quick, Jokey Smurf! Smurf me the long rope there!
Attach the other end to the rocket!
?
BLAM
All set?
Ready!
FIRE!
PSSSIIIIIIIII
FFRRRRRRRSSCCHHHHHHHHHHHHH
7

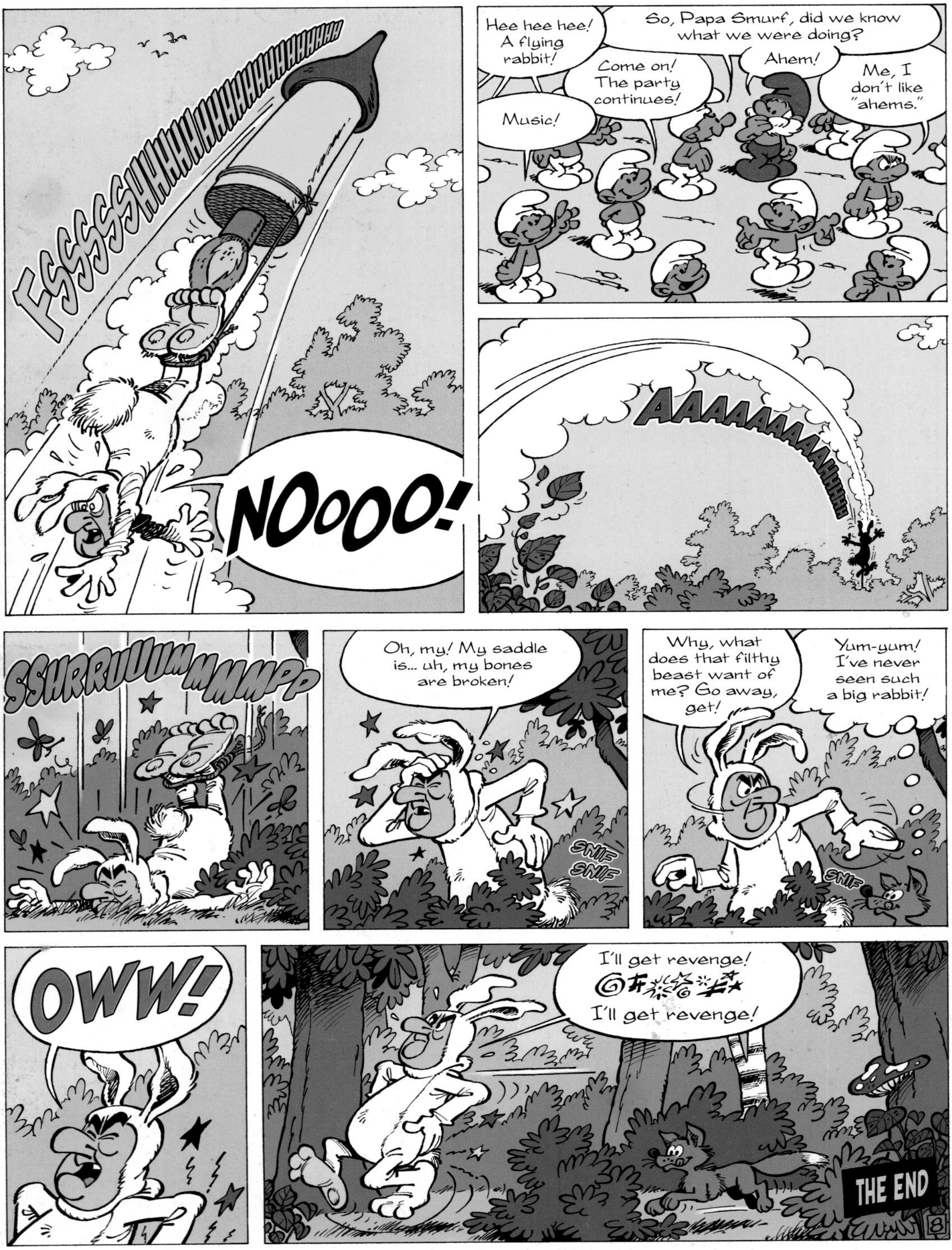
FSSSSSHHHHHHHHHHHHHHHHHHHHHHHHHHHHH
NOOOO!
Hee hee hee! A flying rabbit!
So, Papa Smurf, did we know what we were doing?
Ahem!
Me, I don't like "ahems."
Come on! The party continues!
Music!
AAAAAAAAAAHHHHH
SSHRRUUUMMMMPP
Oh, my! My saddle is... uh, my bones are broken!
SNIF SNIF
Why, what does that filthy beast want of me? Go away, get!
Yum-yum! I've never seen such a big rabbit!
SNIF
OWW!
I'll get revenge!
I'll get revenge!
THE END
8

THE WEATHER-SMURFING MACHINE

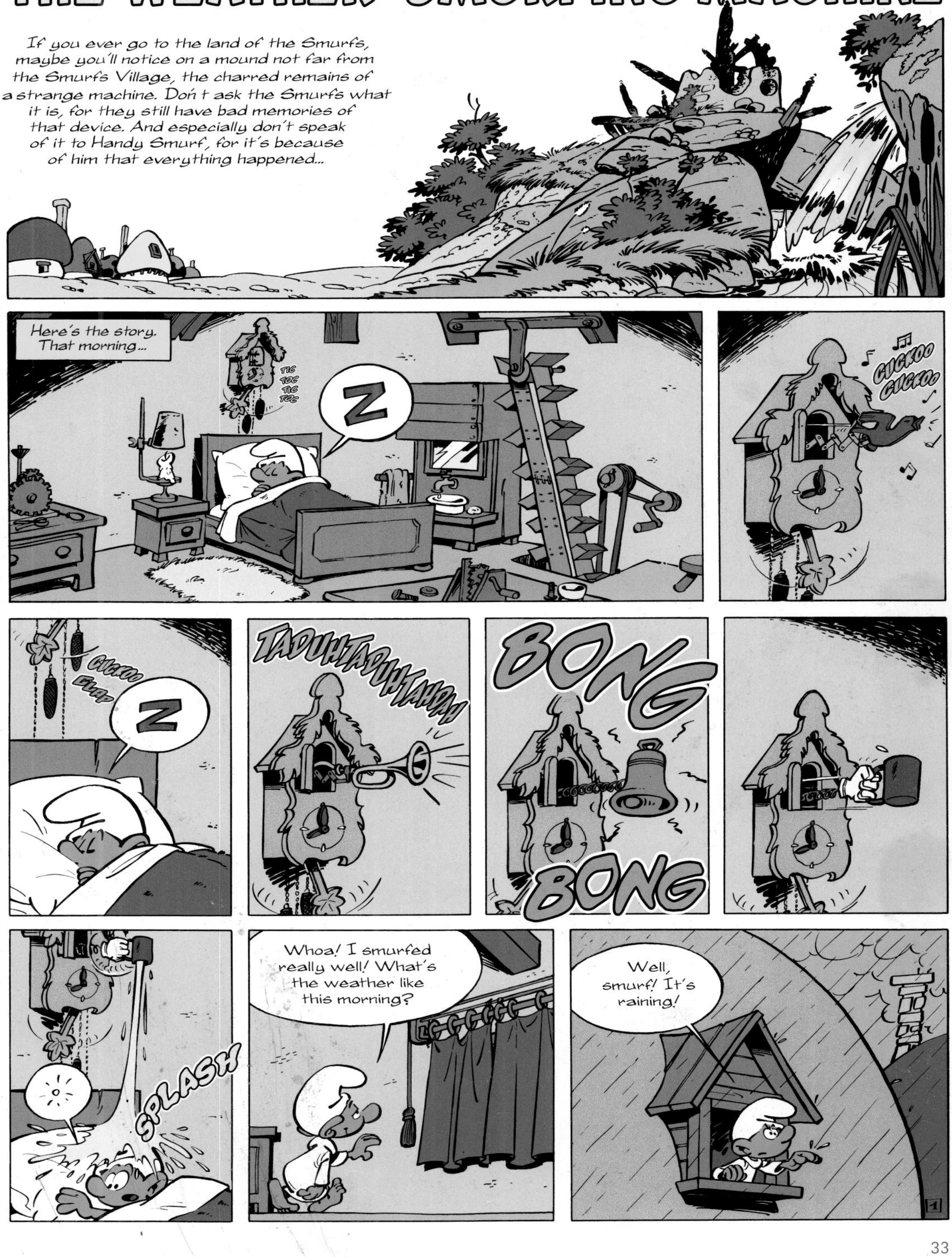
If you ever go to the land of the Smurfs, maybe you'll notice on a mound not far from the Smurfs Village, the charred remains of a strange machine. Don't ask the Smurfs what it is, for they still have bad memories of that device. And especially don't speak of it to Handy Smurf, for it's because of him that everything happened...
Here's the story. That morning...
TIC TOC TIC TOC
Z
CUCKOO CUCKOO
CUCKOO
Z
TADUHTADUHTAHDAH
BONG
BONG
SPLASH
Whoa! I smurfed really well! What's the weather like this morning?
Well, smurf! It's raining!
1

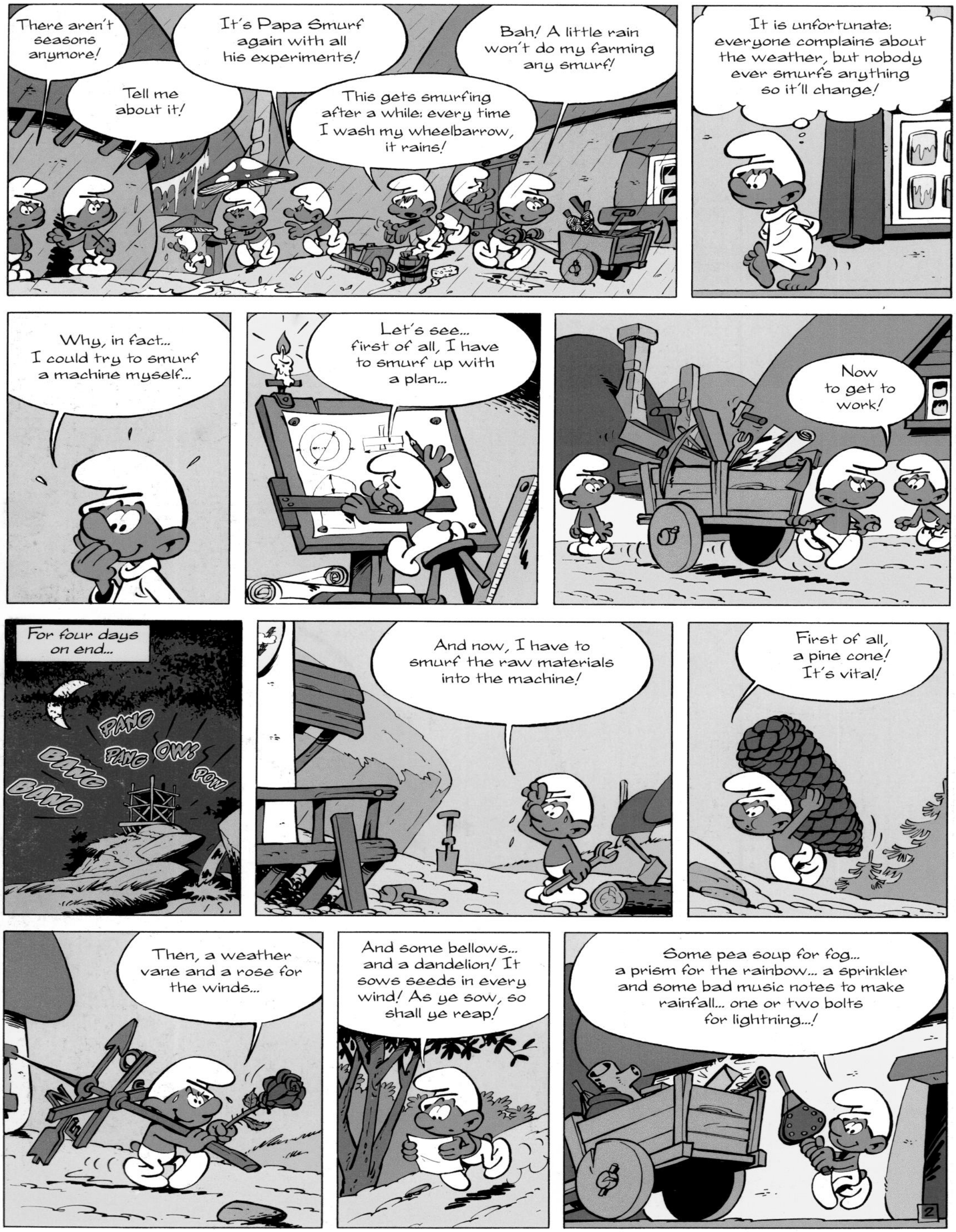
There aren't seasons anymore!
Tell me about it!
It's Papa Smurf again with all his experiments!
This gets smurfing after a while: every time I wash my wheelbarrow, it rains!
Bah! A little rain won't do my farming any smurf!
It is unfortunate: everyone complains about the weather, but nobody ever smurfs anything so it'll change!
Why, in fact... I could try to smurf a machine myself...
Let's see... first of all, I have to smurf up with a plan...
Now to get to work!
For four days on end...
PANG
PANG
OW!
BANG
POW
BANG
And now, I have to smurf the raw materials into the machine!
First of all, a pine cone! It's vital!
Then, a weather vane and a rose for the winds...
And some bellows... and a dandelion! It sows seeds in every wind! As ye sow, so shall ye reap!
Some pea soup for fog... a prism for the rainbow... a sprinkler and some bad music notes to make rainfall... one or two bolts for lightning...!
2

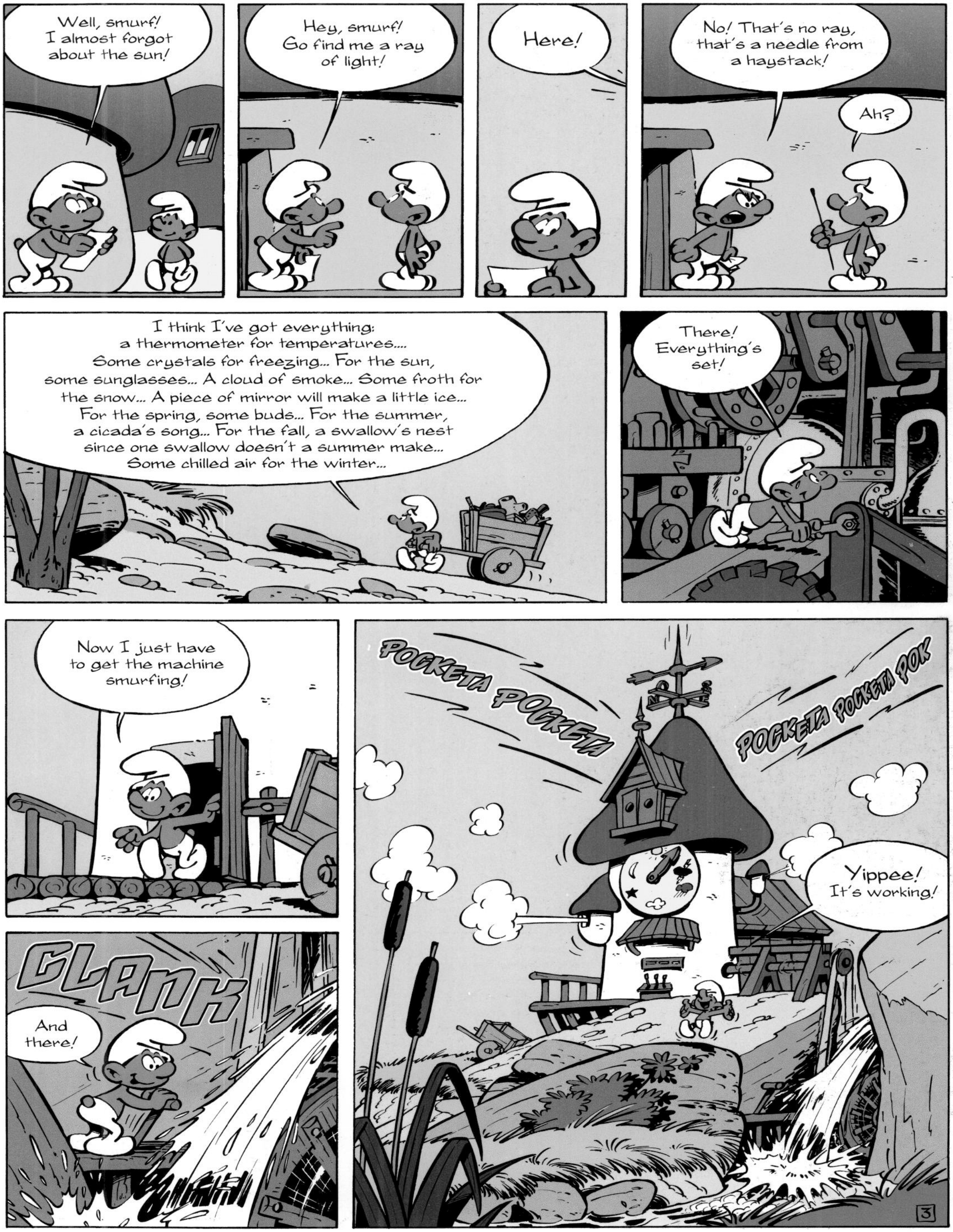

Well, smurf! I almost forgot about the sun!
Hey, smurf! Go find me a ray of light!
Here!
No! That's no ray, that's a needle from a haystack!
Ah?
I think I've got everything: a thermometer for temperatures.... Some crystals for freezing... For the sun, some sunglasses... A cloud of smoke... Some froth for the snow... A piece of mirror will make a little ice... For the spring, some buds... For the summer, a cicada's song... For the fall, a swallow's nest since one swallow doesn't a summer make... Some chilled air for the winter...
There! Everything's set!
Now I just have to get the machine smurfing!
CLANK
And there!
POCKETA POCKETA
POCKETA POCKETA POK
Yippee! It's working!
3

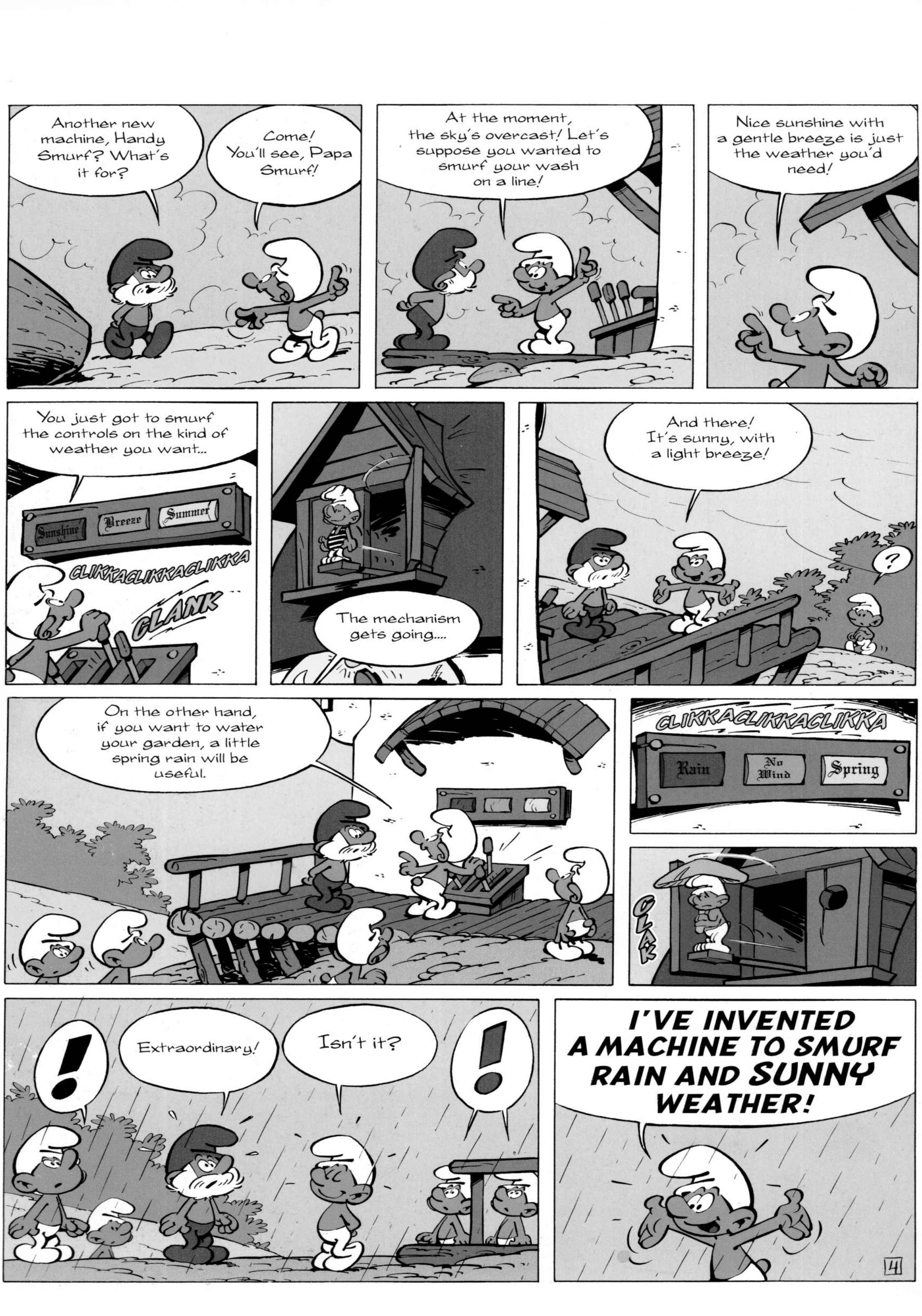

Another new machine, Handy Smurf? What's it for?
Come! You'll see, Papa Smurf!
At the moment, the sky's overcast! Let's suppose you wanted to smurf your wash on a line!
Nice sunshine with a gentle breeze is just the weather you'd need!
You just got to smurf the controls on the kind of weather you want...
Sunshine
Breeze
Summer
CLIKKACLIKKACLIKKA
CLANK
The mechanism gets going....
And there! It's sunny, with a light breeze!
?
On the other hand, if you want to water your garden, a little spring rain will be useful.
CLIKKACLIKKACLIKKA
Rain
No Wind
Spring
CLAK
!
Extraordinary!
Isn't it?
!
I'VE INVENTED A MACHINE TO SMURF RAIN AND SUNNY WEATHER!
4

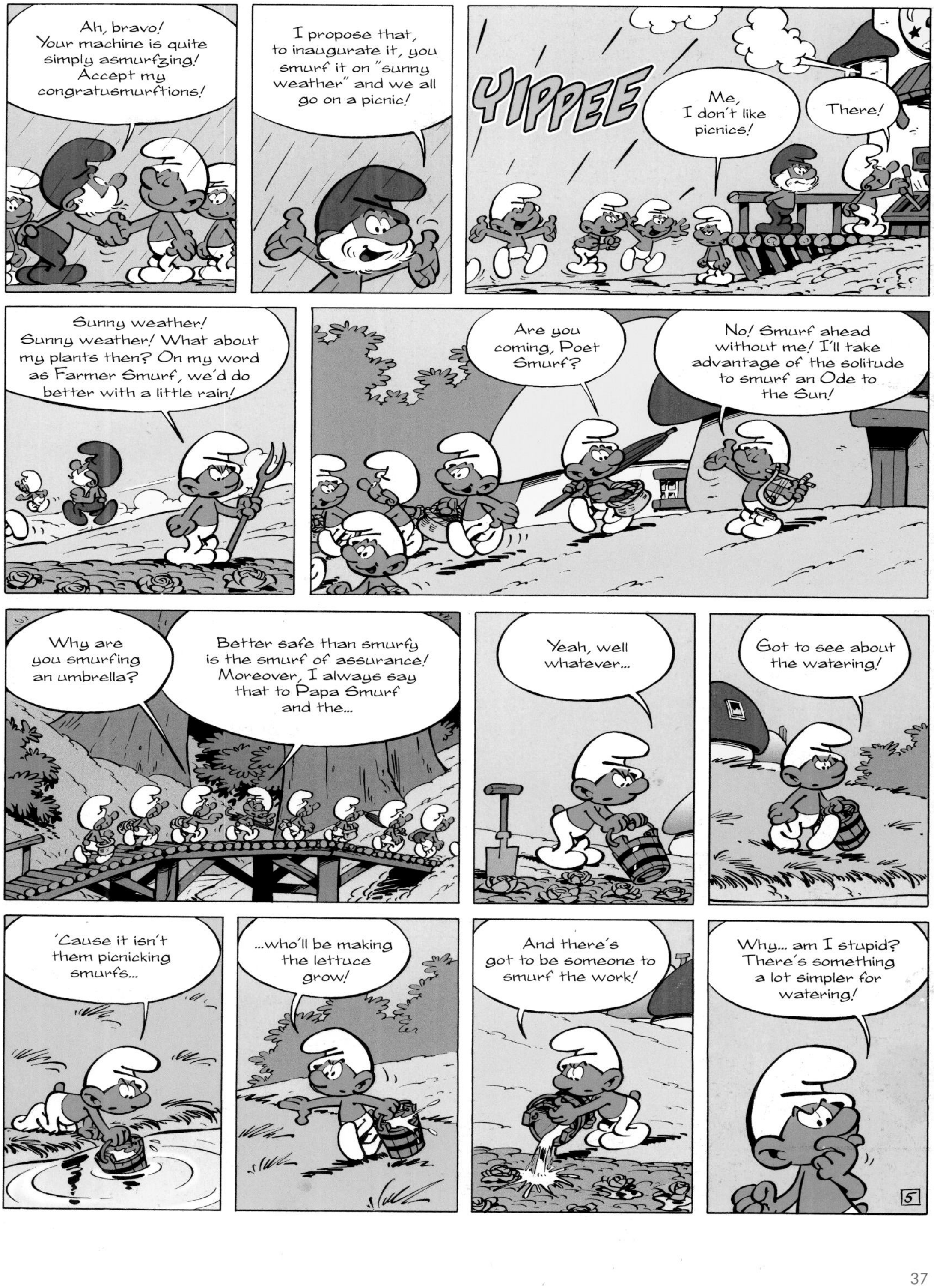
Ah, bravo! Your machine is quite simply asmurfzing! Accept my congratusmurftions!
I propose that, to inaugurate it, you smurf it on "sunny weather" and we all go on a picnic!
YIPPEE
Me, I don't like picnics!
There!
Sunny weather! Sunny weather! What about my plants then? On my word as Farmer Smurf, we'd do better with a little rain!
Are you coming, Poet Smurf?
No! Smurf ahead without me! I'll take advantage of the solitude to smurf an Ode to the Sun!
Why are you smurfing an umbrella?
Better safe than smurfy is the smurf of assurance! Moreover, I always say that to Papa Smurf and the...
Yeah, well whatever...
Got to see about the watering!
'Cause it isn't them picnicking smurfs...
...who'll be making the lettuce grow!
And there's got to be someone to smurf the work!
Why... am I stupid? There's something a lot simpler for watering!
5

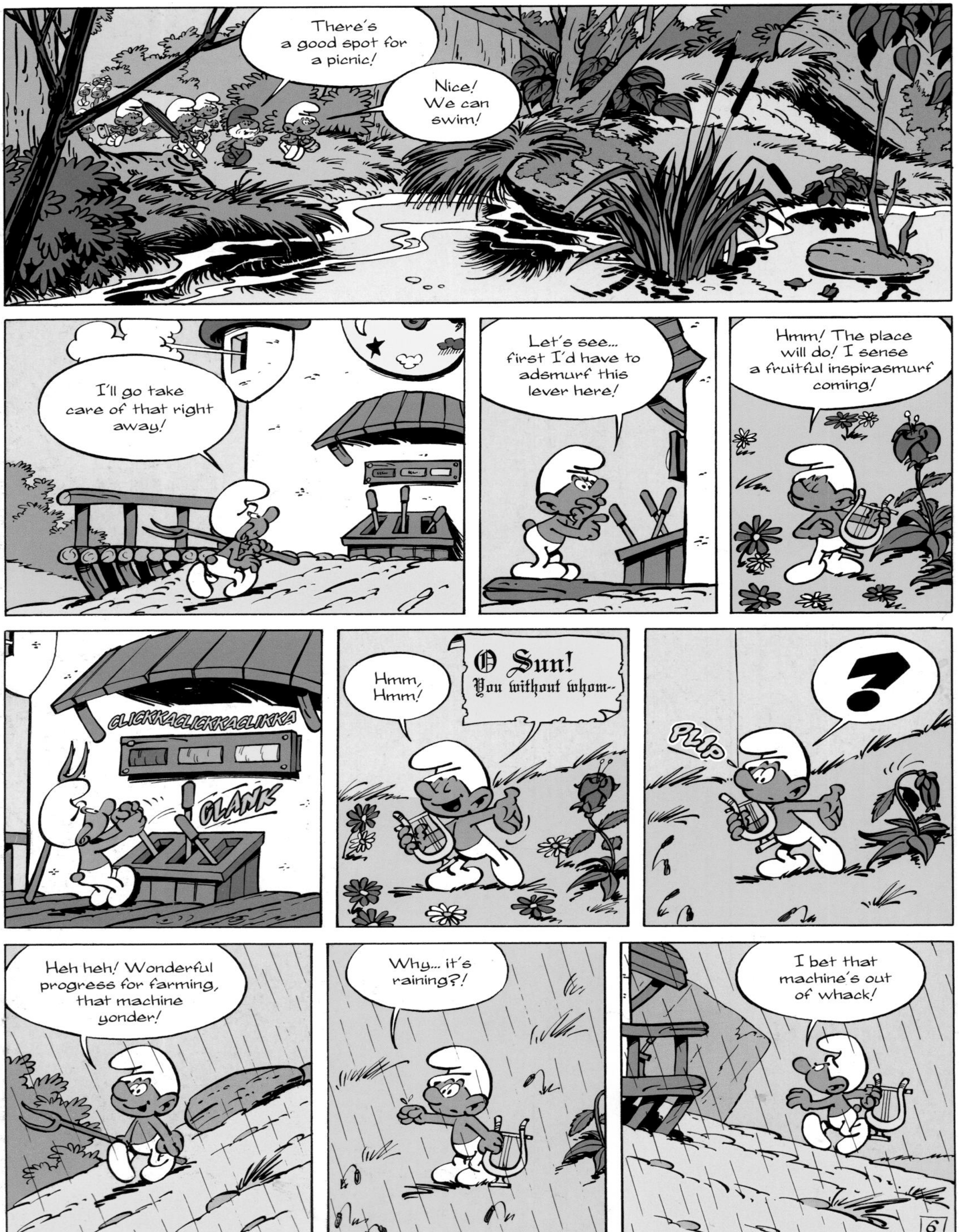
There's a good spot for a picnic!
Nice! We can swim!
I'll go take care of that right away!
Let's see... first I'd have to adsmurf this lever here!
Hmm! The place will do! I sense a fruitful inspirasmurf coming!
CLICKKACLICKKACLIKKA
CLANK
Hmm, Hmm!
O Sun! You without whom--
PLIP
?
Heh heh! Wonderful progress for farming, that machine yonder!
Why... it's raining?!
I bet that machine's out of whack!
6

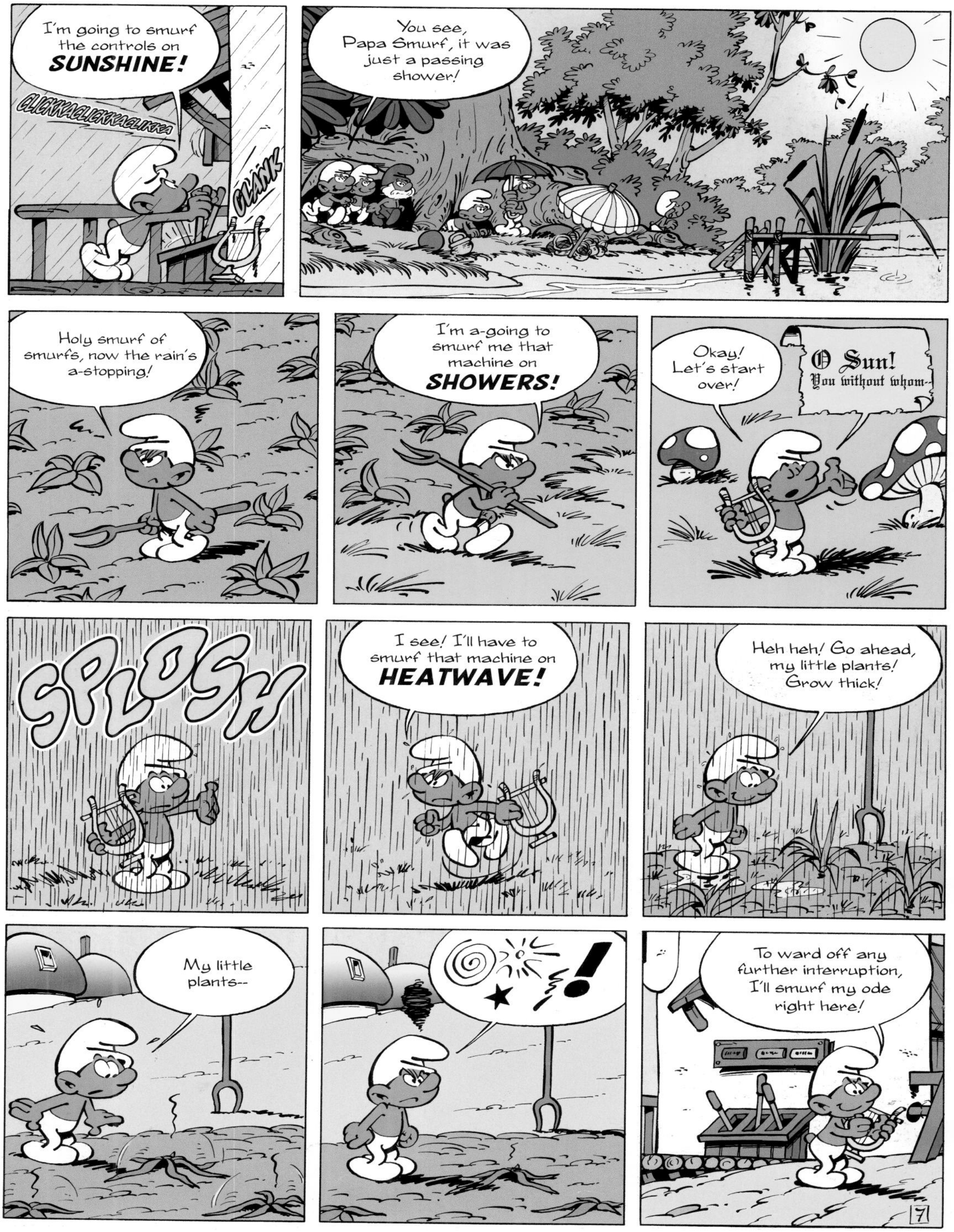
I'm going to smurf the controls on SUNSHINE!
CLICKKACLICKKACLIKKA
CLANK
You see, Papa Smurf, it was just a passing shower!
Holy smurf of smurfs, now the rain's a-stopping!
I'm a-going to smurf me that machine on SHOWERS!
Okay! Let's start over!
O Sun! You without whom--
SPLOSH
I see! I'll have to smurf that machine on HEATWAVE!
Heh heh! Go ahead, my little plants! Grow thick!
My little plants--
!
To ward off any further interruption, I'll smurf my ode right here!
7

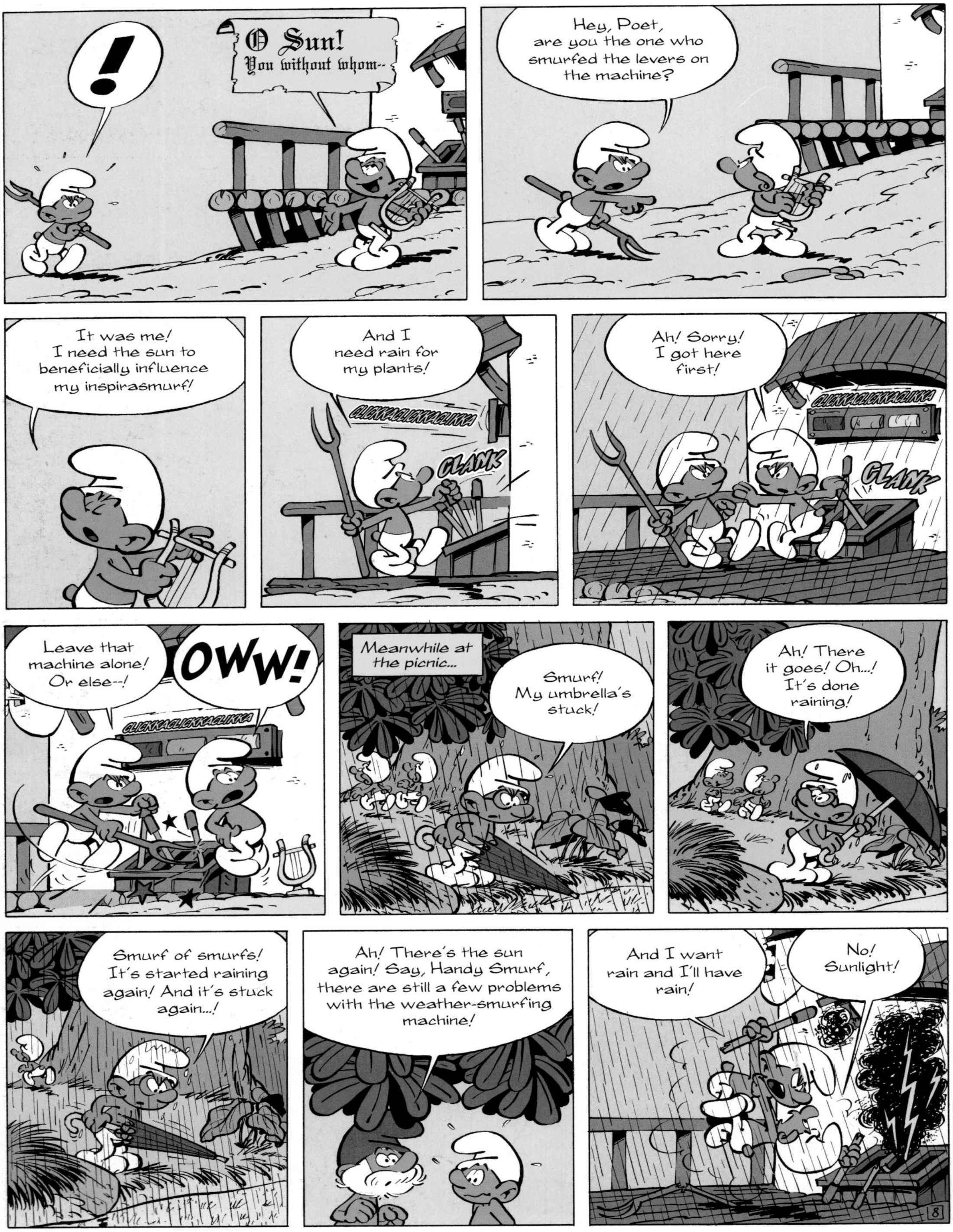
!
O Sun! You without whom--
Hey, Poet, are you the one who smurfed the levers on the machine?
It was me! I need the sun to beneficially influence my inspirasmurf!
And I need rain for my plants!
CLICKKACLICKKACLIKKA
CLANK
Ah! Sorry! I got here first!
CLICKKACLICKKACLIKKA
CLANK
Leave that machine alone! Or else--!
OWW!
CLICKKACLICKKACLIKKA
Meanwhile at the picnic...
Smurf! My umbrella's stuck!
Ah! There it goes! Oh...! It's done raining!
Smurf of smurfs! It's started raining again! And it's stuck again...!
Ah! There's the sun again! Say, Handy Smurf, there are still a few problems with the weather-smurfing machine!
And I want rain and I'll have rain!
No! Sunlight!
8

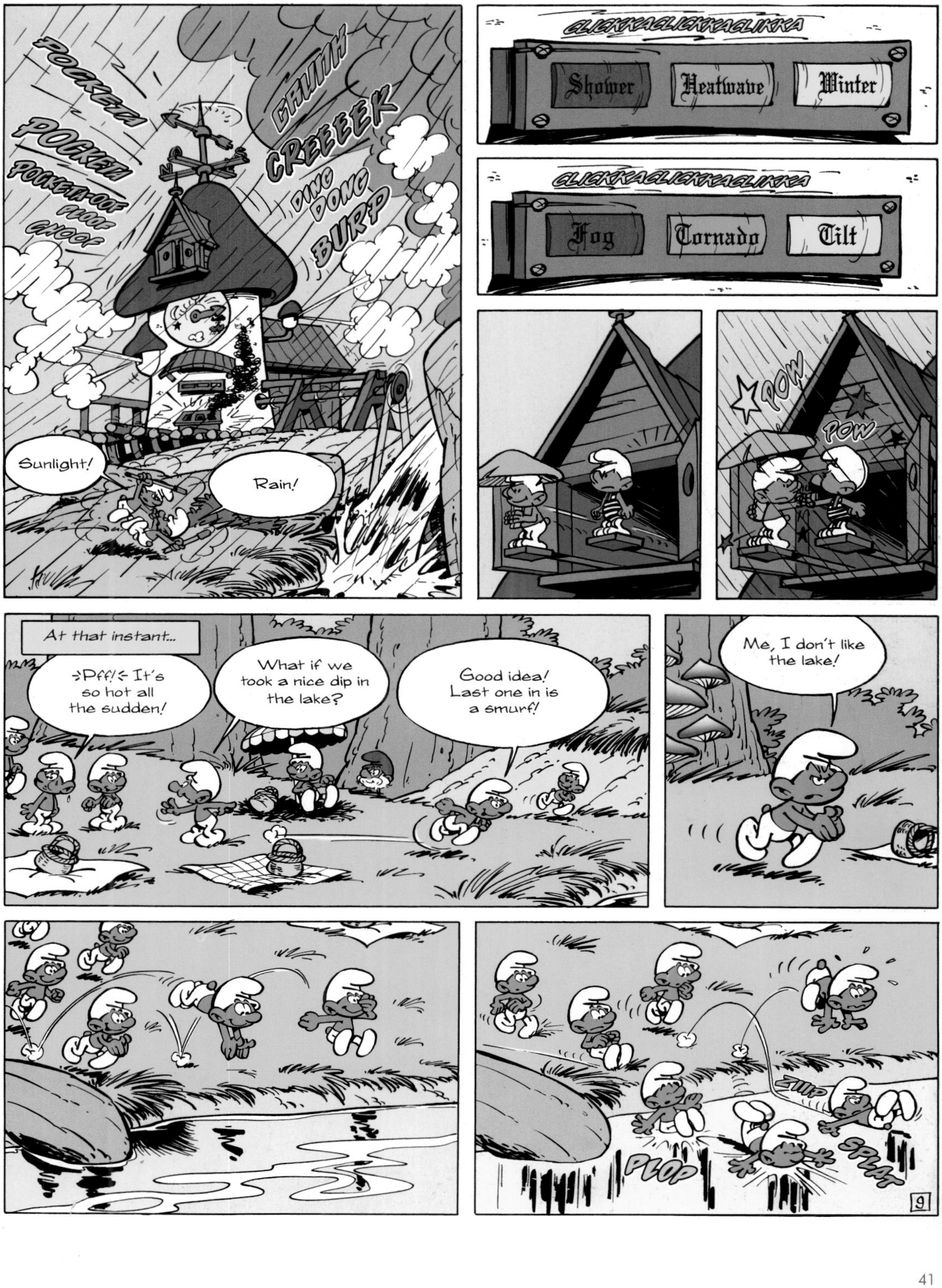
POCKETA
POCKETA
POCKETA-OOF
PLOOF
GHOOF
GRUNK
CREEEEK
DING
DONG
BURP
Sunlight!
Rain!
CLICKKACLICKKACLIKKA
Shower
Heatwave
Winter
CLICKKACLICKKACLIKKA
Fog
Tornado
Tilt
POW
POW
At that instant...
Pff! It's so hot all the sudden!
What if we took a nice dip in the lake?
Good idea! Last one in is a smurf!
Me, I don't like the lake!
ZUIP
PLOP
SPLAT
9

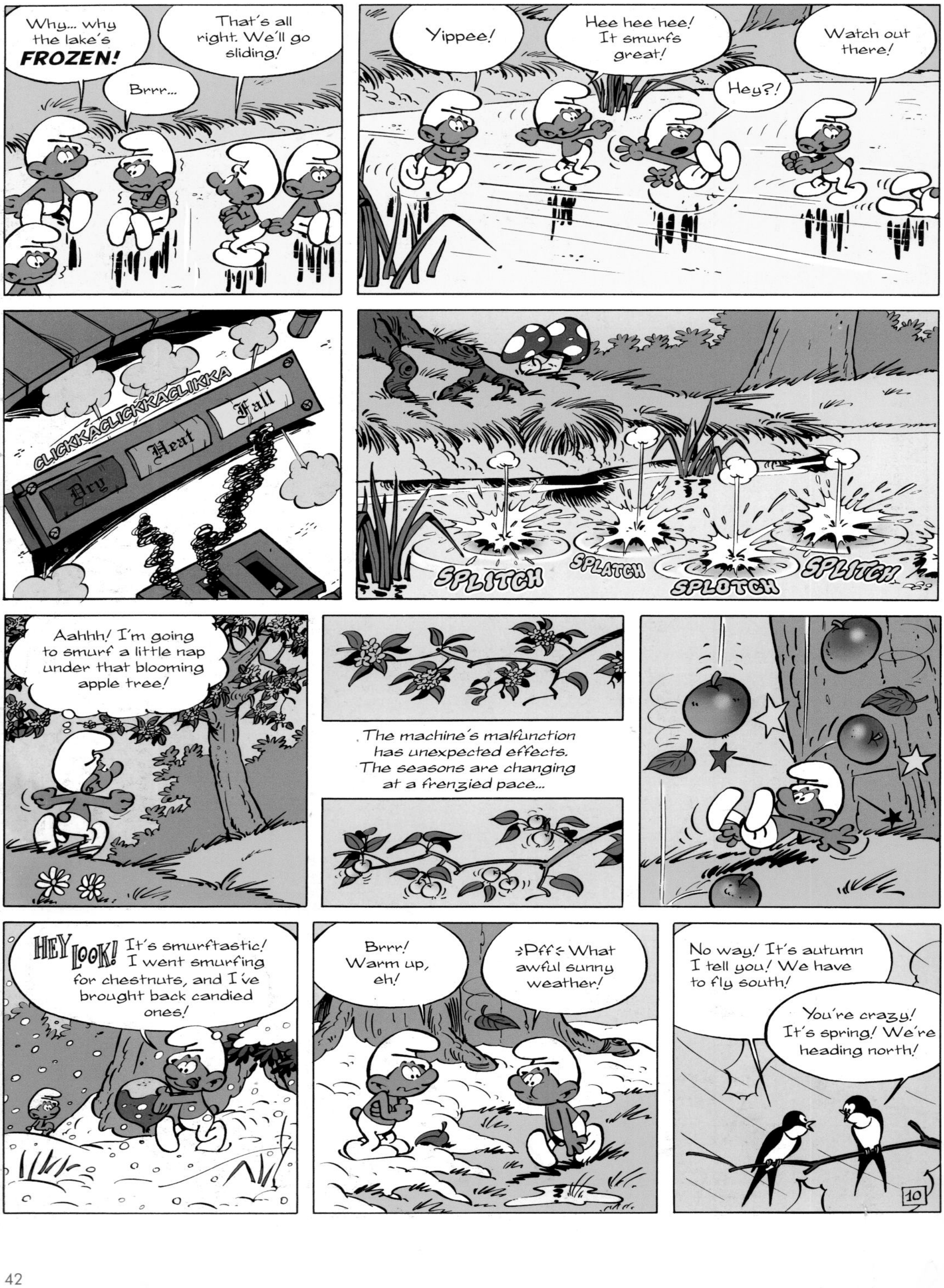

Why... why the lake's **FROZEN!**
Brrr...
That's all right. We'll go sliding!
Yippee!
Hee hee hee! It smurfs great!
Hey?!
Watch out there!
CLICKKACLICKKACLICKKA
Dry
Heat
Fall
SPLITCH
SPLATCH
SPLOTCH
SPLITCH
Aahhh! I'm going to smurf a little nap under that blooming apple tree!
The machine's malfunction has unexpected effects. The seasons are changing at a frenzied pace...
HEY LOOK! It's smurftastic! I went smurfing for chestnuts, and I've brought back candied ones!
Brrr! Warm up, eh!
Pff What awful sunny weather!
No way! It's autumn I tell you! We have to fly south!
You're crazy! It's spring! We're heading north!
10

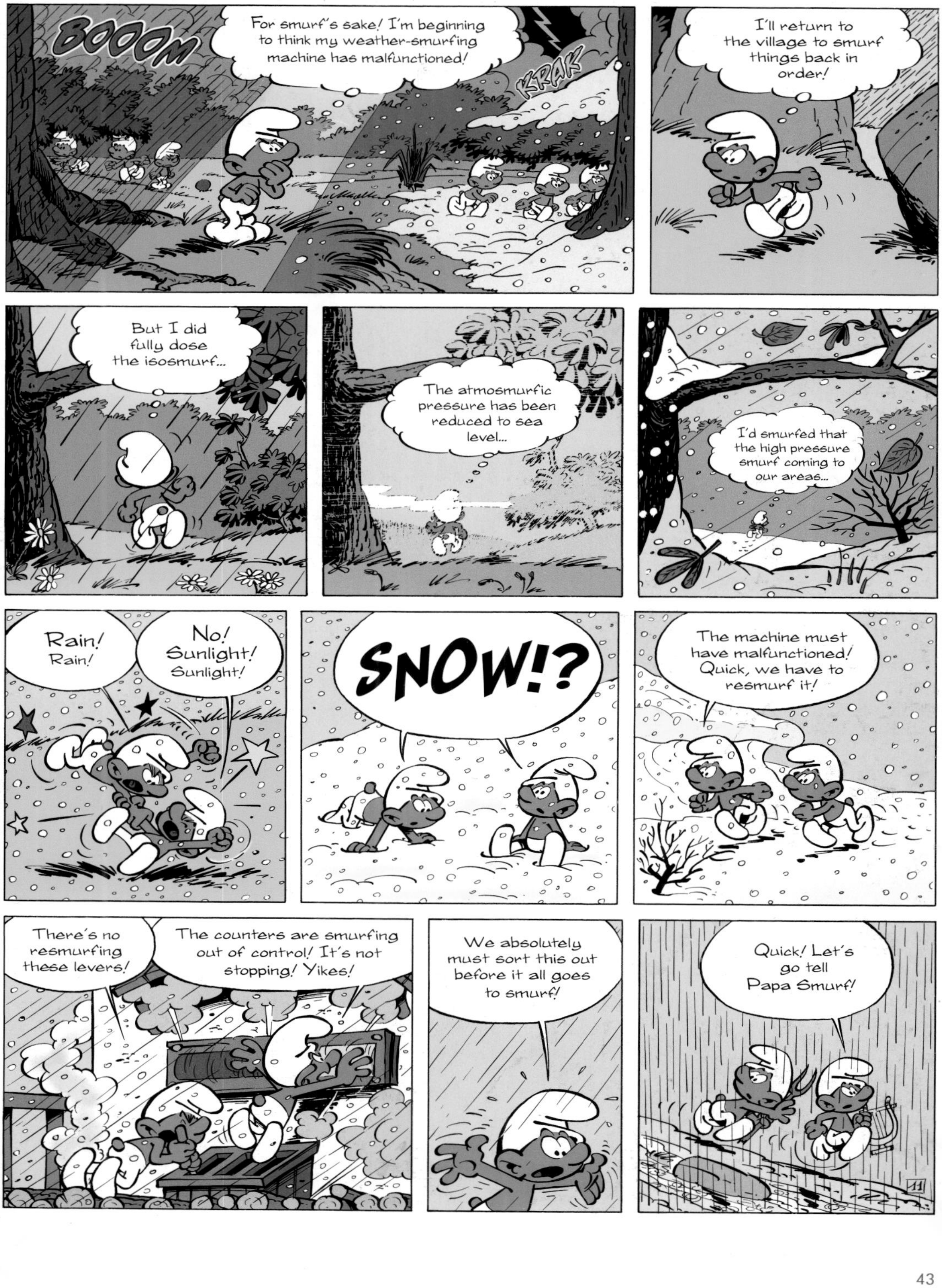
BOOOM
For smurf's sake! I'm beginning to think my weather-smurfing machine has malfunctioned!
KRAK
I'll return to the village to smurf things back in order!
But I did fully dose the isosmurf...
The atmosmurfic pressure has been reduced to sea level...
I'd smurfed that the high pressure smurf coming to our areas...
Rain! Rain!
No! Sunlight! Sunlight!
SNOW!?
The machine must have malfunctioned! Quick, we have to resmurf it!
There's no resmurfing these levers!
The counters are smurfing out of control! It's not stopping! Yikes!
We absolutely must sort this out before it all goes to smurf!
Quick! Let's go tell Papa Smurf!
11

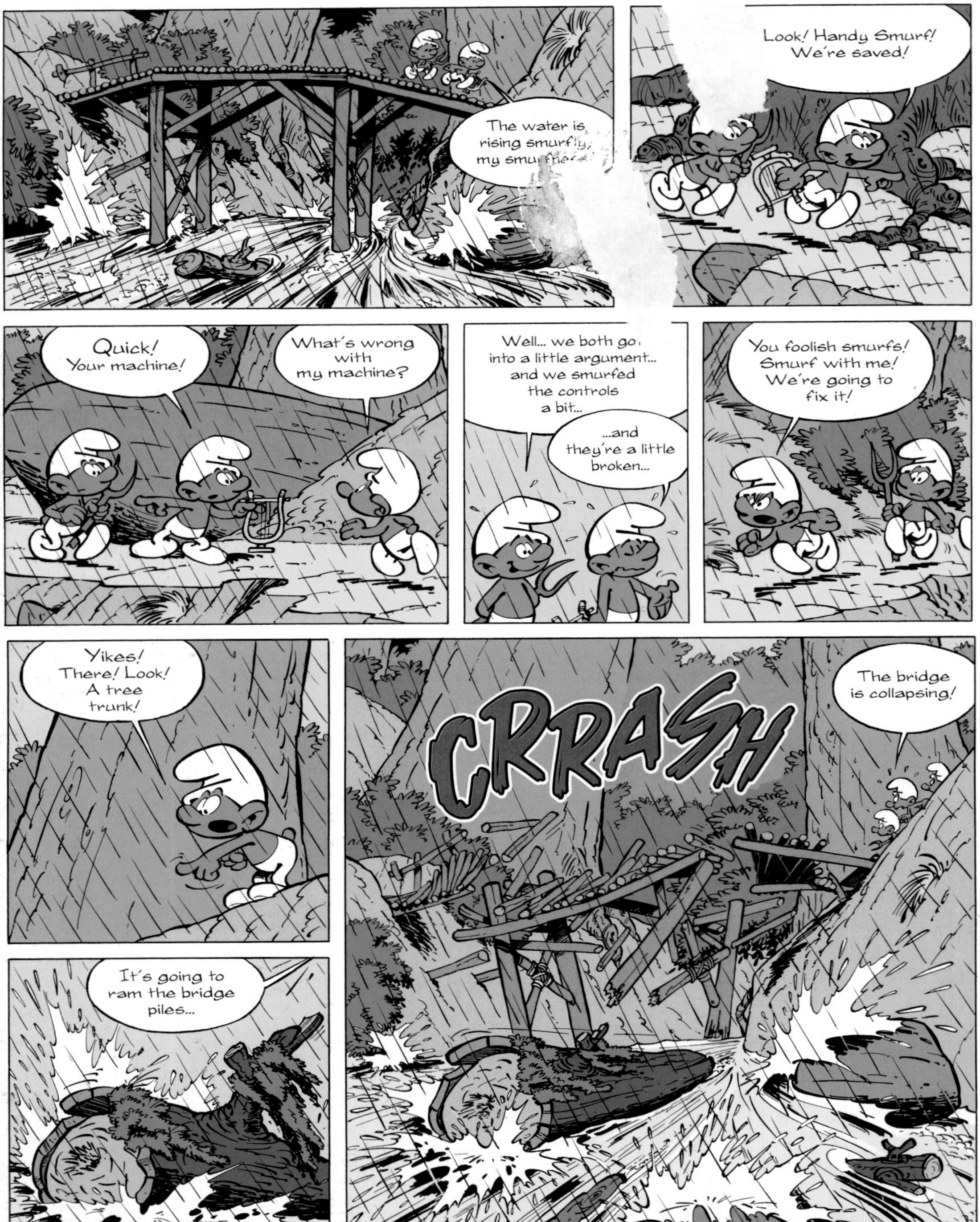
The water is rising smurfly, my smurfie...
Look! Handy Smurf! We're saved!
Quick! Your machine!
What's wrong with my machine?
Well... we both got into a little argument... and we smurfed the controls a bit...
...and they're a little broken...
You foolish smurfs! Smurf with me! We're going to fix it!
Yikes! There! Look! A tree trunk!
It's going to ram the bridge piles...
CRRASH
The bridge is collapsing!
12

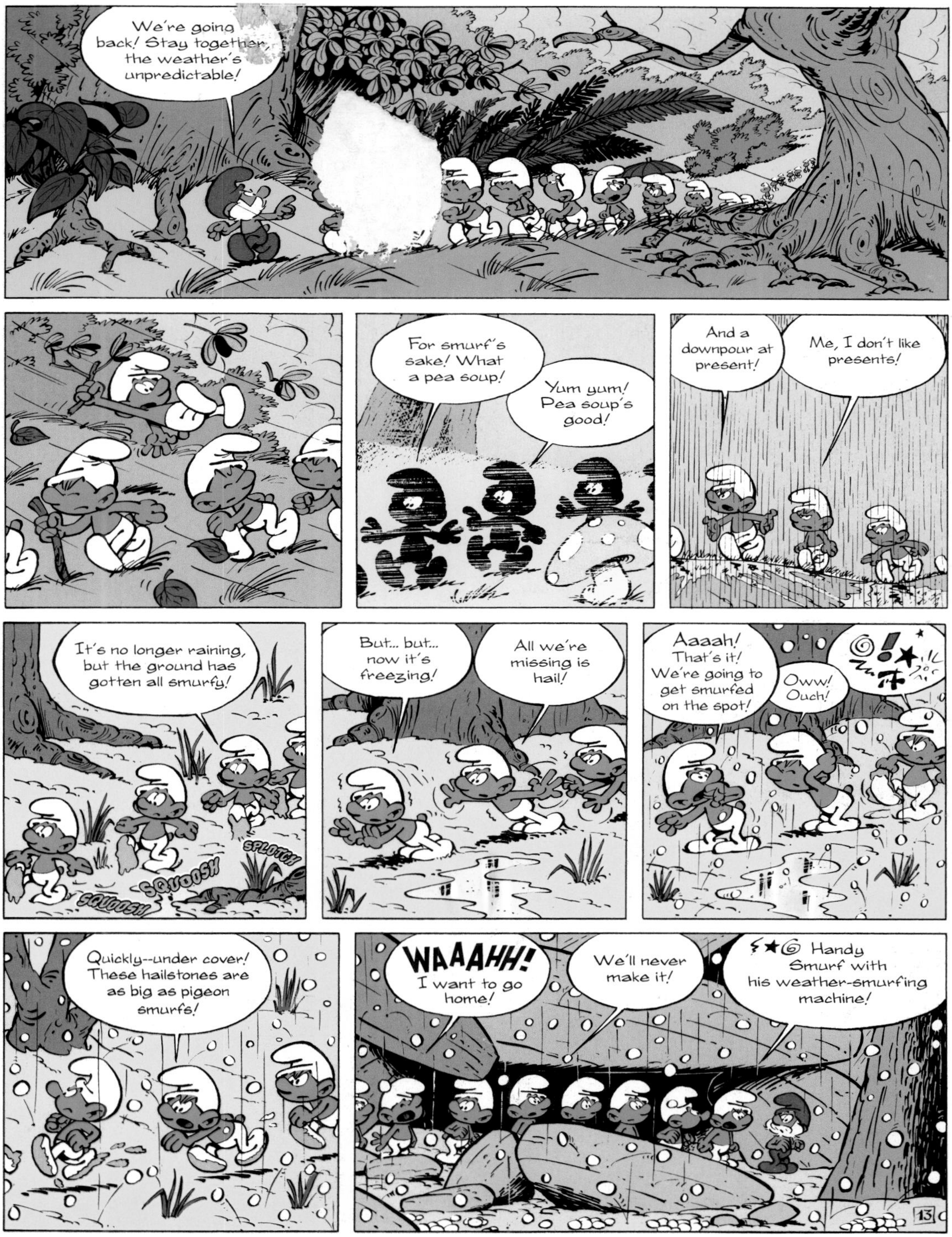

We're going back! Stay together, the weather's unpredictable!
For smurf's sake! What a pea soup!
Yum yum! Pea soup's good!
And a downpour at present!
Me, I don't like presents!
It's no longer raining, but the ground has gotten all smurfy!
SPLOTCH
SQUOOSH
SQUOOSH
But... but... now it's freezing!
All we're missing is hail!
Aaaah! That's it! We're going to get smurfed on the spot!
Oww! Ouch!
Quickly--under cover! These hailstones are as big as pigeon smurfs!
WAAAHH! I want to go home!
We'll never make it!
Handy Smurf with his weather-smurfing machine!
13

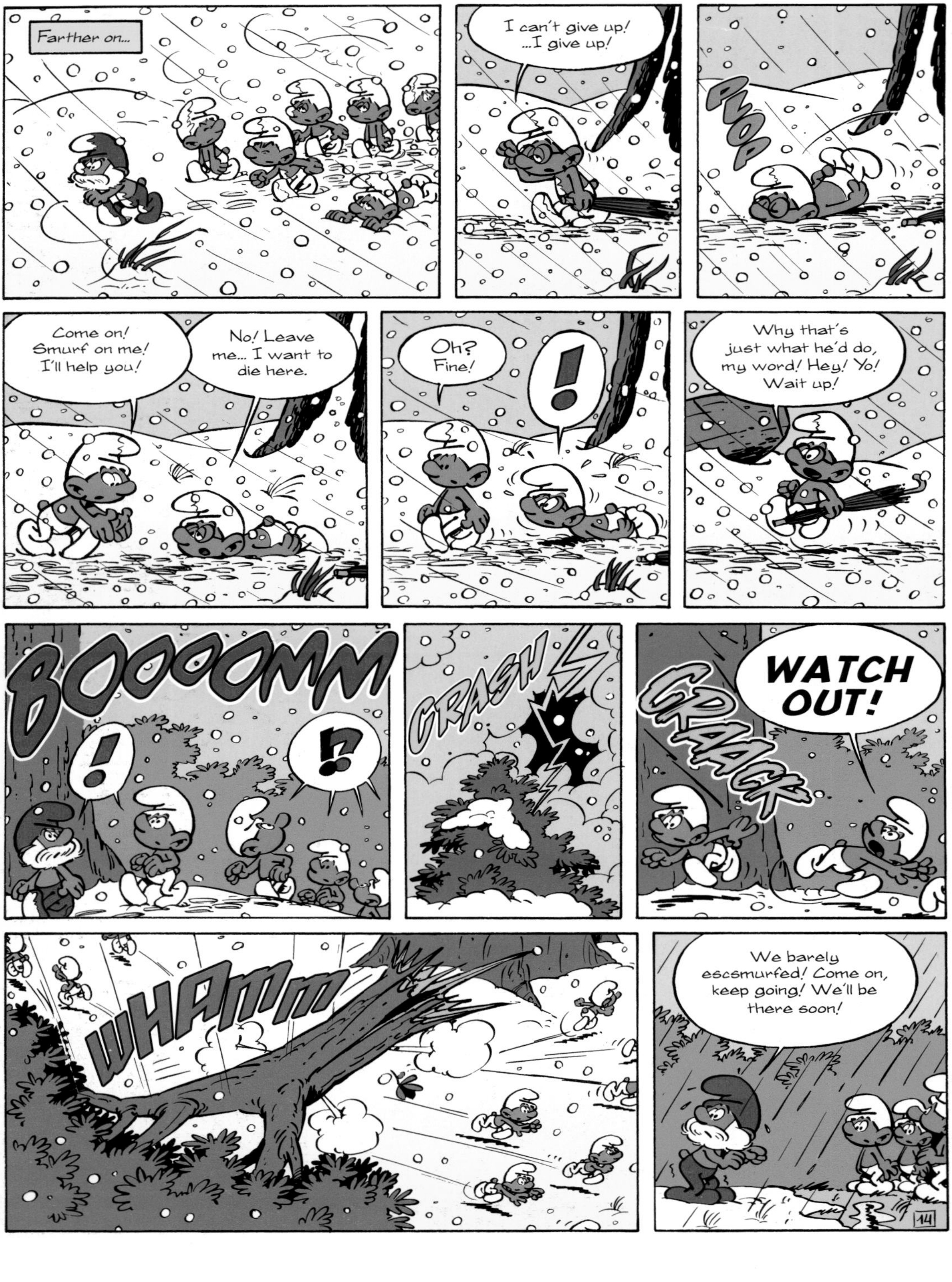
Farther on...
I can't give up! ...I give up!
PLOP
Come on! Smurf on me! I'll help you!
No! Leave me... I want to die here.
Oh? Fine!
!
Why that's just what he'd do, my word! Hey! Yo! Wait up!
BOOOOMM
!
!?
CRASH
CRAACK
WATCH OUT!
WHAMM
We barely escsmurfed! Come on, keep going! We'll be there soon!
14

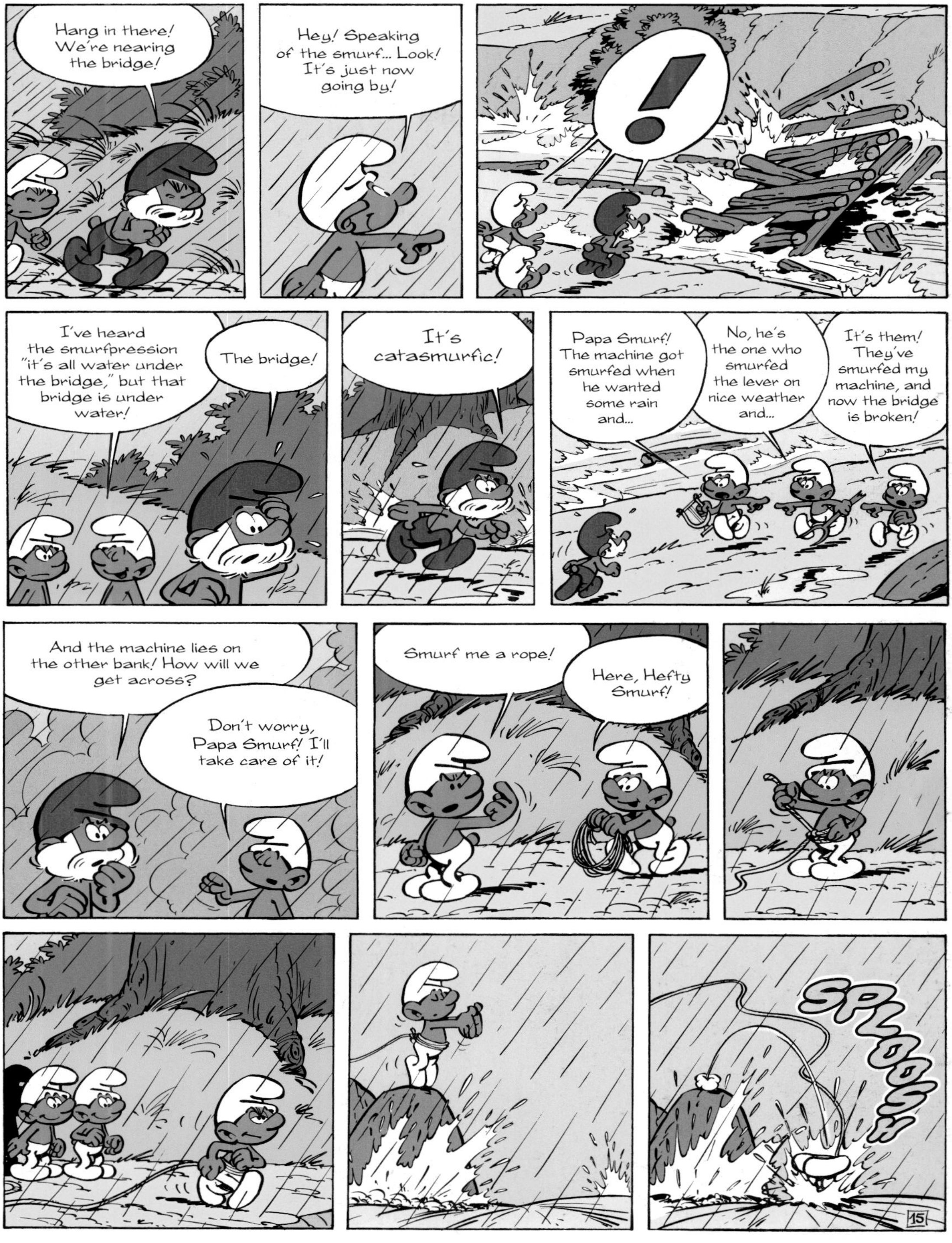
Hang in there! We're nearing the bridge!
Hey! Speaking of the smurf... Look! It's just now going by!
!
I've heard the smurfpression "it's all water under the bridge," but that bridge is under water!
The bridge!
It's catasmurfic!
Papa Smurf! The machine got smurfed when he wanted some rain and...
No, he's the one who smurfed the lever on nice weather and...
It's them! They've smurfed my machine, and now the bridge is broken!
And the machine lies on the other bank! How will we get across?
Don't worry, Papa Smurf! I'll take care of it!
Smurf me a rope!
Here, Hefty Smurf!
SPLOOSH
15

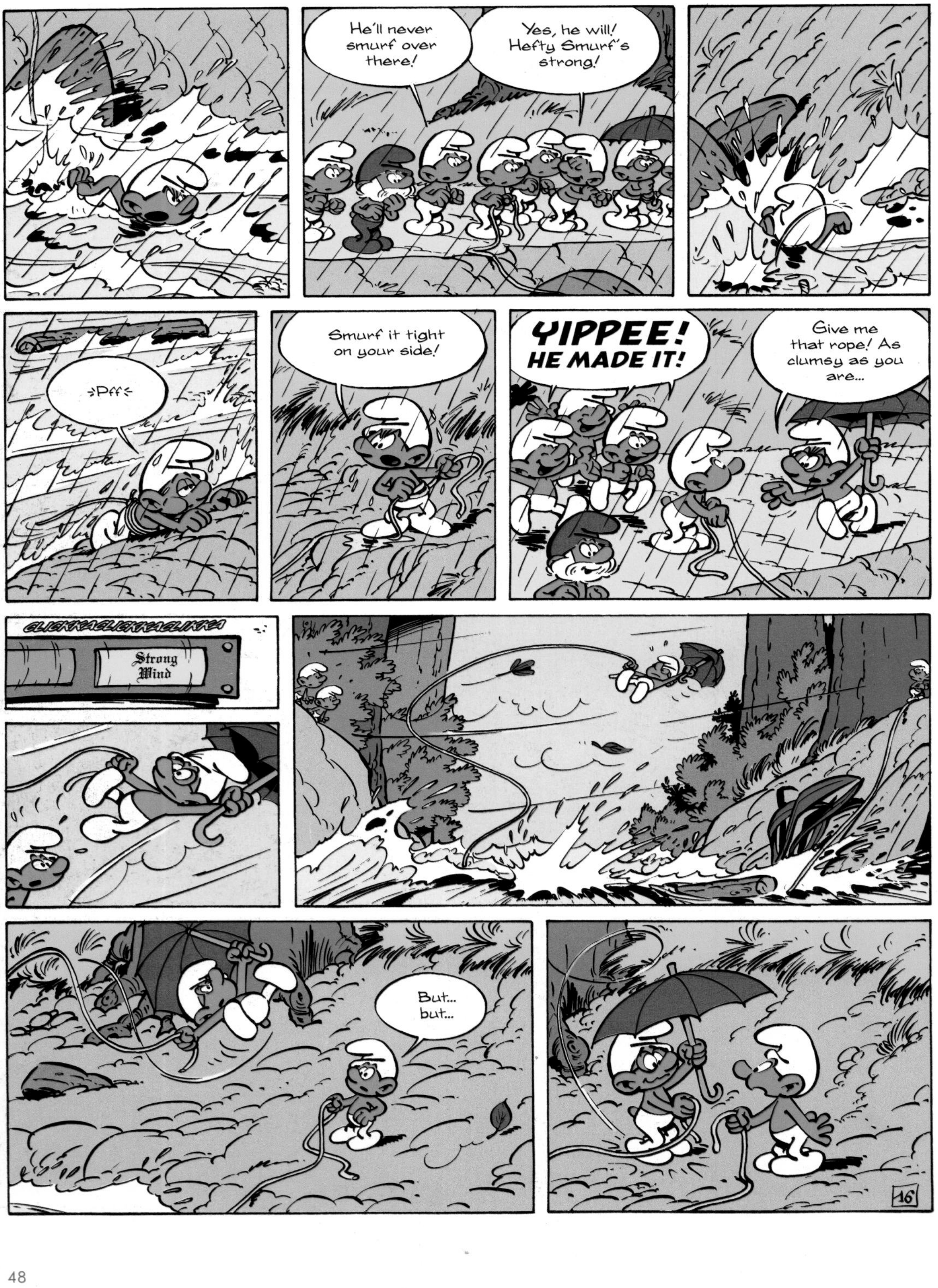

He'll never smurf over there!
Yes, he will! Hefty Smurf's strong!
Pff
Smurf it tight on your side!
YIPPEE! HE MADE IT!
Give me that rope! As clumsy as you are...
CLICKKACLICKKACLIKKA
Strong Wind
But... but...
16

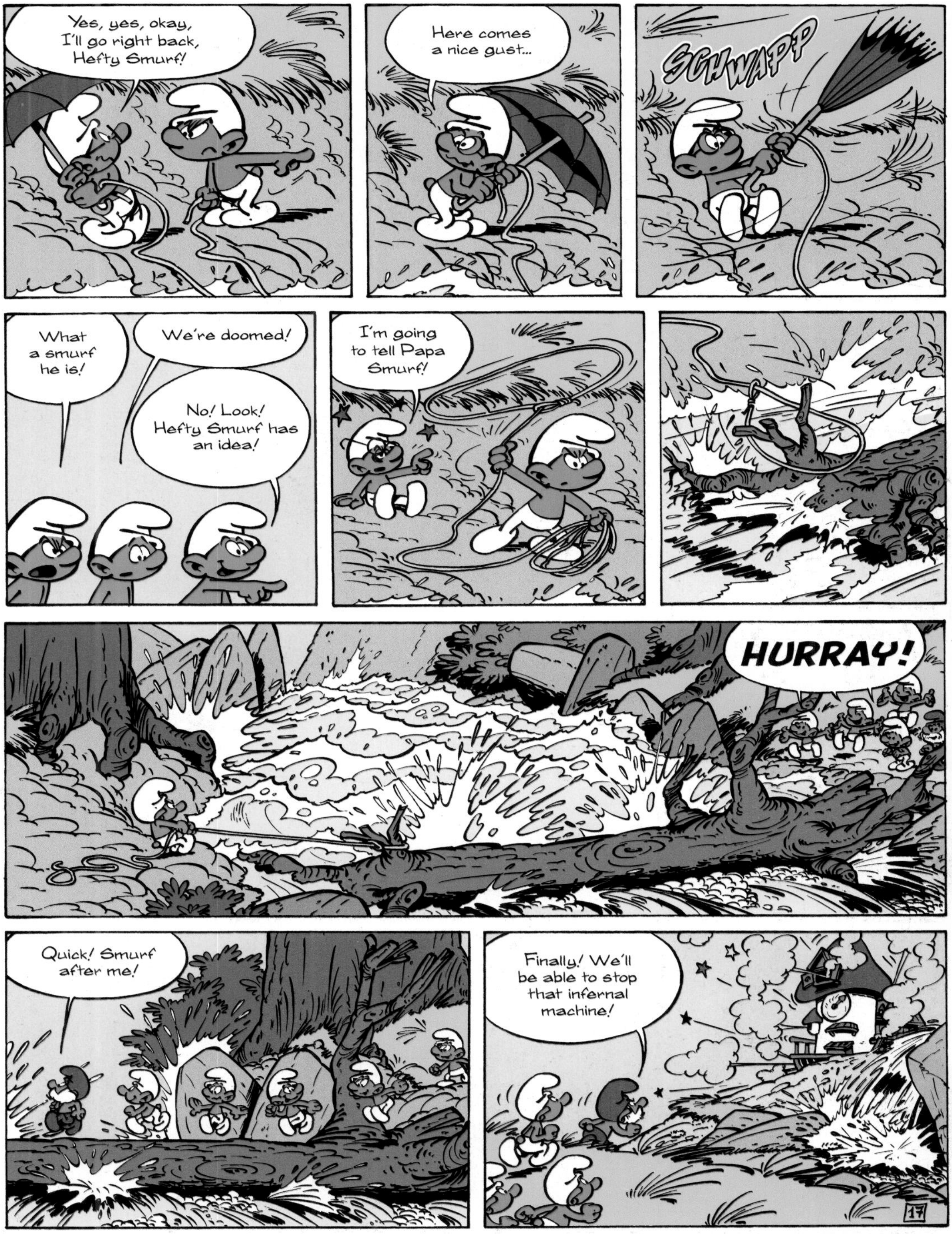
Yes, yes, okay, I'll go right back, Hefty Smurf!
Here comes a nice gust...
SCHWAPP
What a smurf he is!
We're doomed!
No! Look! Hefty Smurf has an idea!
I'm going to tell Papa Smurf!
HURRAY!
Quick! Smurf after me!
Finally! We'll be able to stop that infernal machine!
17

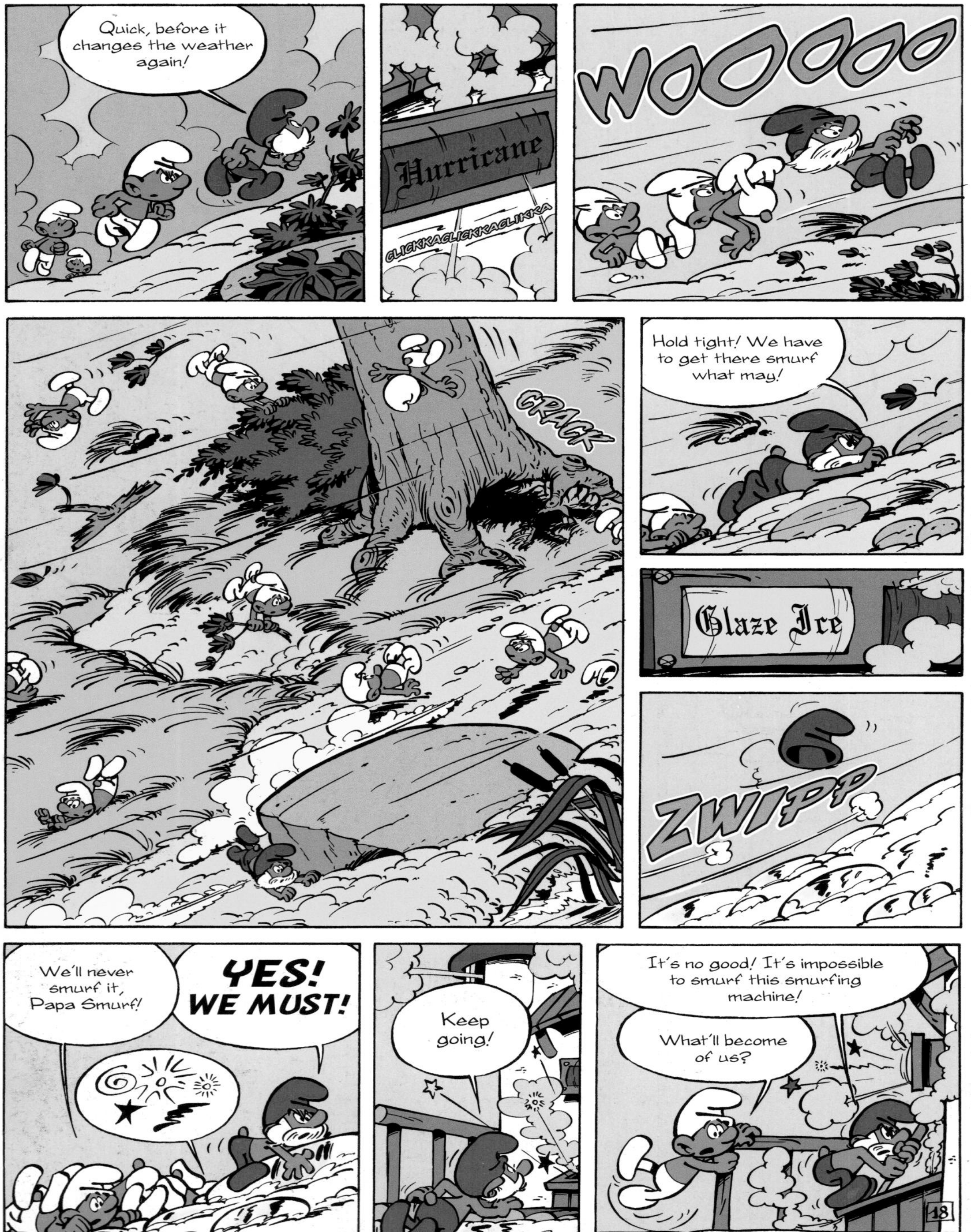
Quick, before it changes the weather again!
Hurricane
CLICKKACLICKKACLIKKA
WOOOOOO
CRACK
Hold tight! We have to get there smurf what may!
Glaze Ice
ZWIPP
We'll never smurf it, Papa Smurf!
YES! WE MUST!
Keep going!
It's no good! It's impossible to smurf this smurfing machine!
What'll become of us?
18

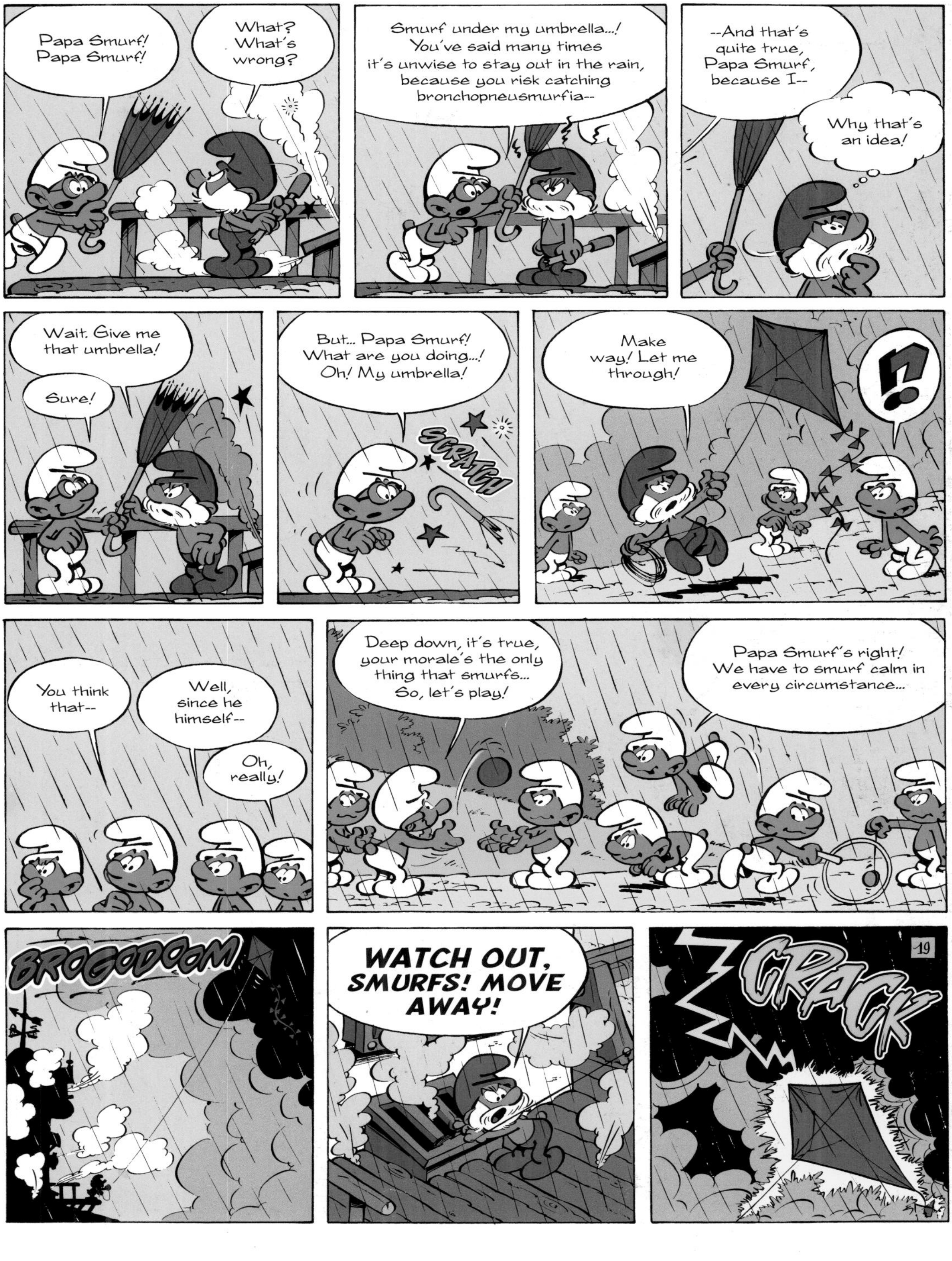

Papa Smurf! Papa Smurf!
What? What's wrong?
Smurf under my umbrella...! You've said many times it's unwise to stay out in the rain, because you risk catching bronchopneusmurfia--
--And that's quite true, Papa Smurf, because I--
Why that's an idea!
Wait. Give me that umbrella!
Sure!
But... Papa Smurf! What are you doing...! Oh! My umbrella!
SCRATCH
Make way! Let me through!
You think that--
Well, since he himself--
Oh, really!
Deep down, it's true, your morale's the only thing that smurfs... So, let's play!
Papa Smurf's right! We have to smurf calm in every circumstance...
BROGODOOM
WATCH OUT, SMURFS! MOVE AWAY!
19
CRACK

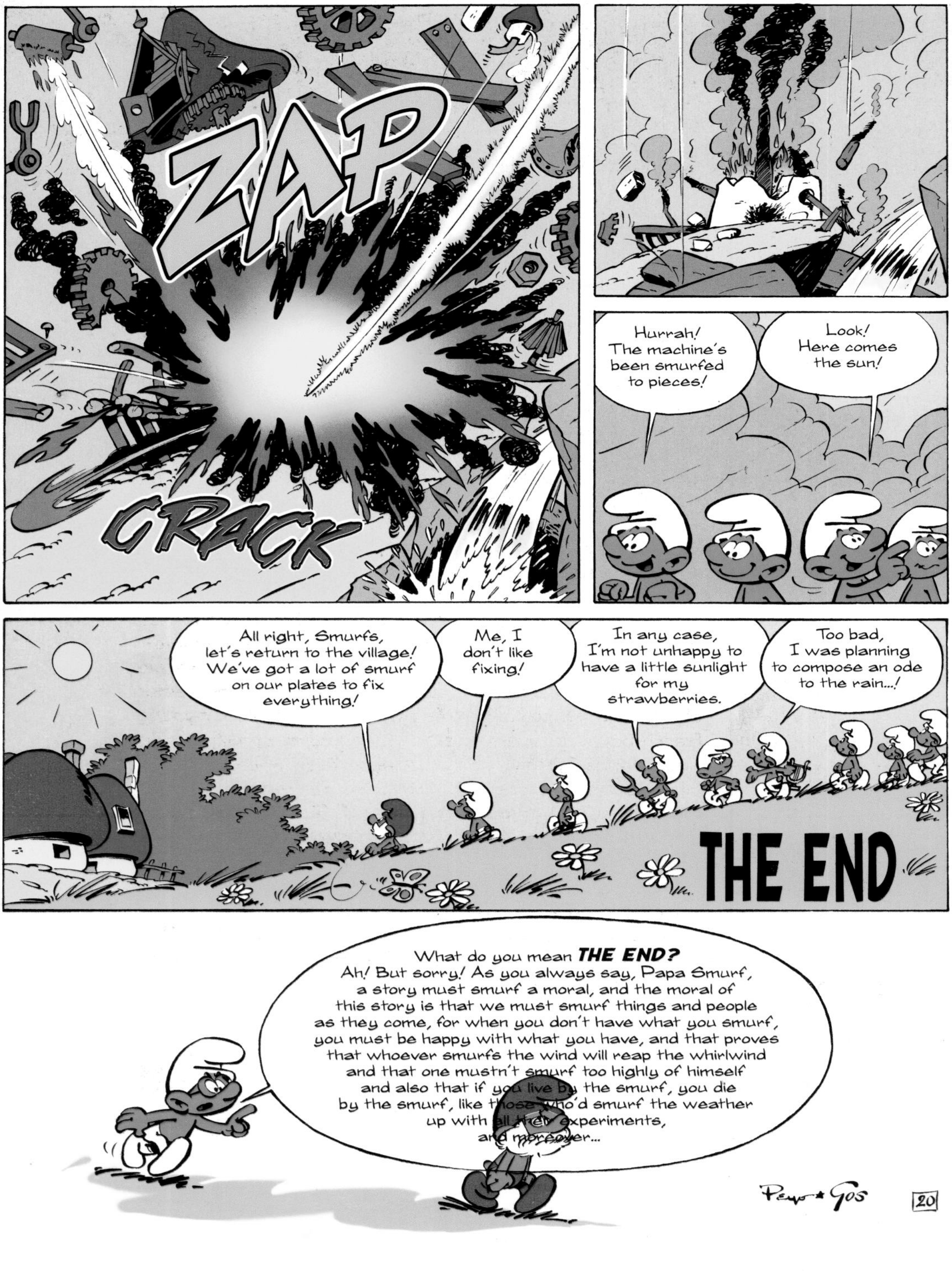
ZAP
CRACK
Hurrah! The machine's been smurfed to pieces!
Look! Here comes the sun!
All right, Smurfs, let's return to the village! We've got a lot of smurf on our plates to fix everything!
Me, I don't like fixing!
In any case, I'm not unhappy to have a little sunlight for my strawberries.
Too bad, I was planning to compose an ode to the rain...!
THE END
What do you mean THE END? Ah! But sorry! As you always say, Papa Smurf, a story must smurf a moral, and the moral of this story is that we must smurf things and people as they come, for when you don't have what you smurf, you must be happy with what you have, and that proves that whoever smurfs the wind will reap the whirlwind and that one mustn't smurf too highly of himself and also that if you live by the smurf, you die by the smurf, like those who'd smurf the weather up with all their experiments, and moreover...
Peyo ★ Gos
20

WATCH OUT FOR PAPERCUTZ™

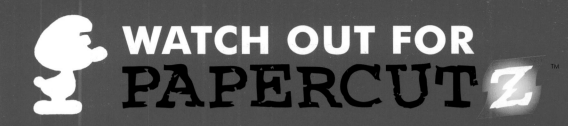

Welcome to the creatively fertile fourteenth SMURFS graphic novel by Peyo from Papercutz, the little company dedicated to publishing great graphic novels for all ages. I'm Jim Salicrup, the Smurf-in-Chief that refuses to change diapers.

Wow! You'd think that an event as exciting as the birth of a new Smurf would be THE major Smurf event of any year, and ordinarily, you'd be right. But, this year, there are so many exciting events happening, it may just make your head Smurf!

The biggest news is that Smurfs 2 will be opening soon at a theater near you on August 3, 2013. That's right, the sequel to the first smash Smurfs movie is coming out this year, featuring all the stars you loved from the first film in an all-new sequel set in France!

But that's not all! To celebrate the release of the new film, Papercutz has a couple of exciting projects also coming your way. We'll just tell you about one of them now, and announce the other in SMURFS #15. After all, we realize there's only so much Smurf-excitement a mere human can possibly handle.

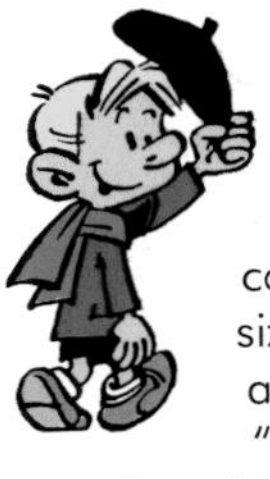

So, are you ready? Papercutz is proud to announce we will be publishing a new graphic novel series from Peyo, the creator of THE SMURFS, called BENNY BREAKIRON. It's about a young French boy with super-powers. "When I came up with Benny, I soon decided to give him an Achilles heel: when he gets a cold he loses all his strength," explained Peyo about his pint-size powerhouse. A far-too-brief sample of BENNY BREAKIRON, appears on the following pages, and BENNY BREAKIRON #1 "The Red Taxis" will be available soon at booksellers everywhere.

A Smurf Baby, a Smurf sequel, and a new Papercutz graphic novel series by Peyo—how exciting is that? If all that wasn't enough Smurfiness for you, then whatever you do, wherever you go, don't miss THE SMURFS #15 "The Smurflings," for the story that introduces even more young Smurfs, as well as another big SMURFS announcement!

Smurf you later!

Jim

THE RED TAXIS

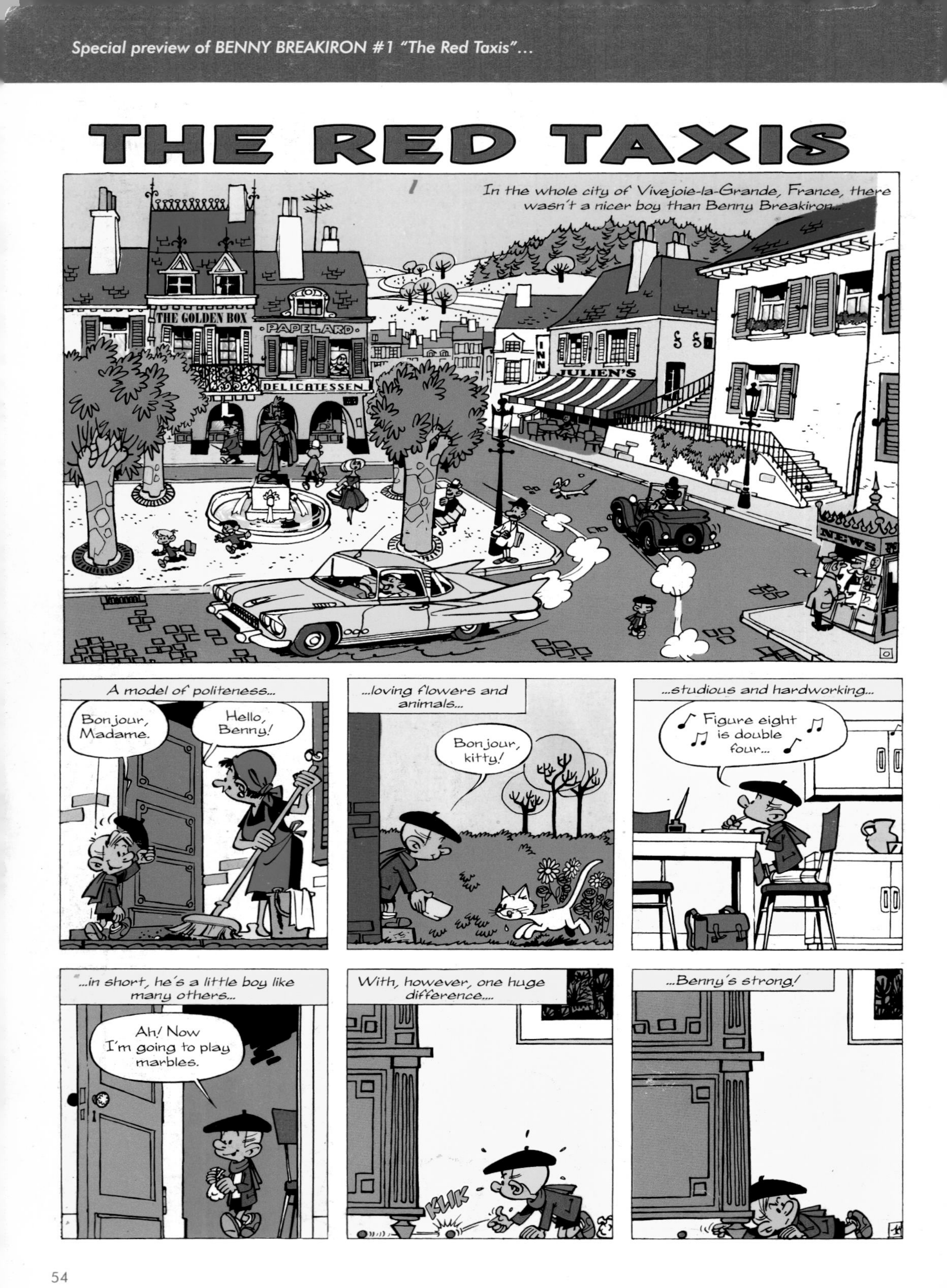
In the whole city of Vivejoie-la-Grande, France, there wasn't a nicer boy than Benny Breakiron...
THE GOLDEN BOX
PAPELARD
DELICATESSEN
INN
JULIEN'S
NEWS
A model of politeness...
Bonjour, Madame.
Hello, Benny!
...loving flowers and animals...
Bonjour, kitty!
...studious and hardworking...
Figure eight is double four...
...in short, he's a little boy like many others...
Ah! Now I'm going to play marbles.
With, however, one huge difference....
KLIK
...Benny's strong!

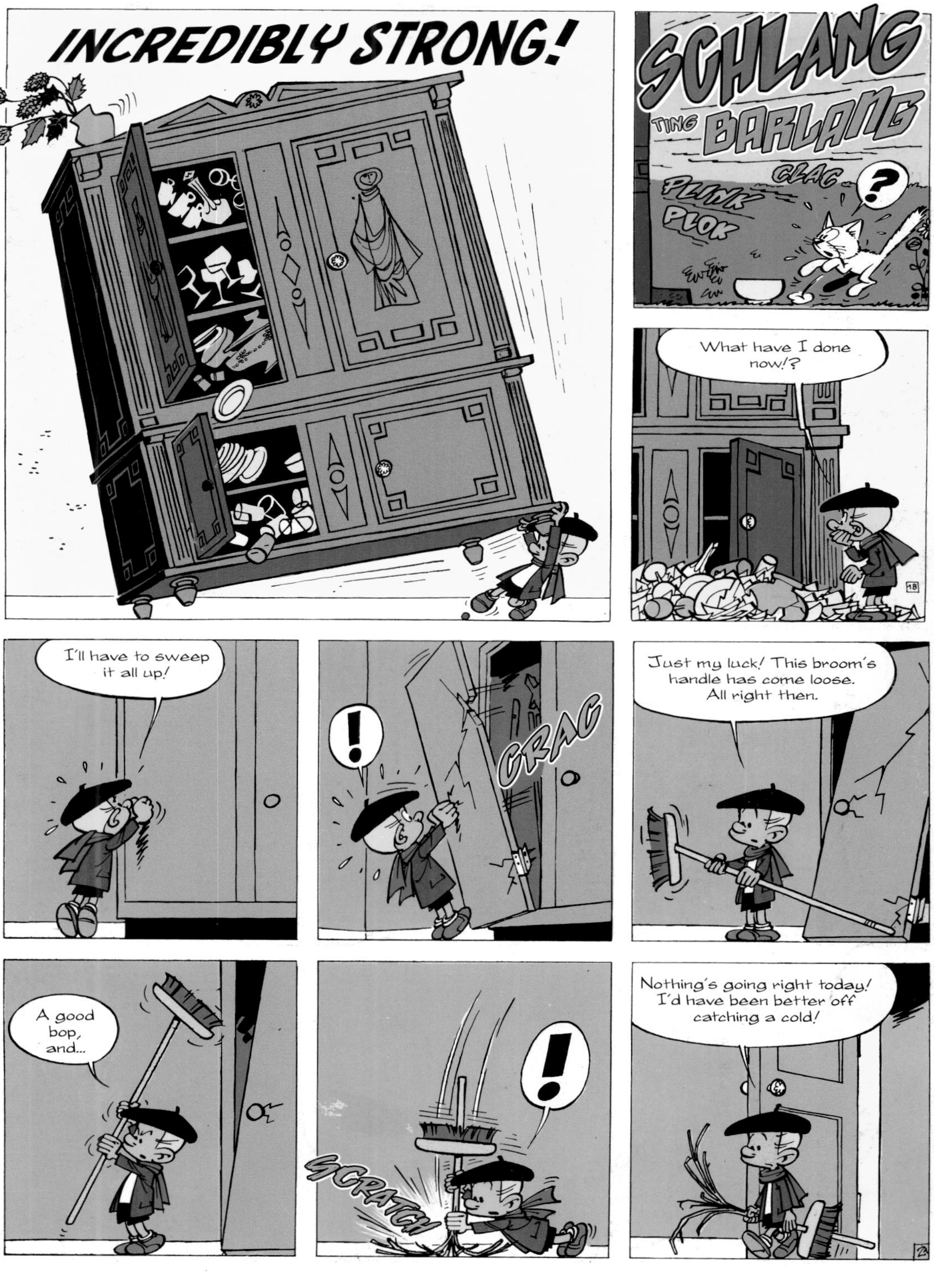

INCREDIBLY STRONG!
SCHLANG
TING BARLANG
CLAC
PLINK
PLOK
?
What have I done now!?
I'll have to sweep it all up!
!
CRAC
Just my luck! This broom's handle has come loose. All right then.
A good bop, and...
!
SCRATCH
Nothing's going right today! I'd have been better off catching a cold!

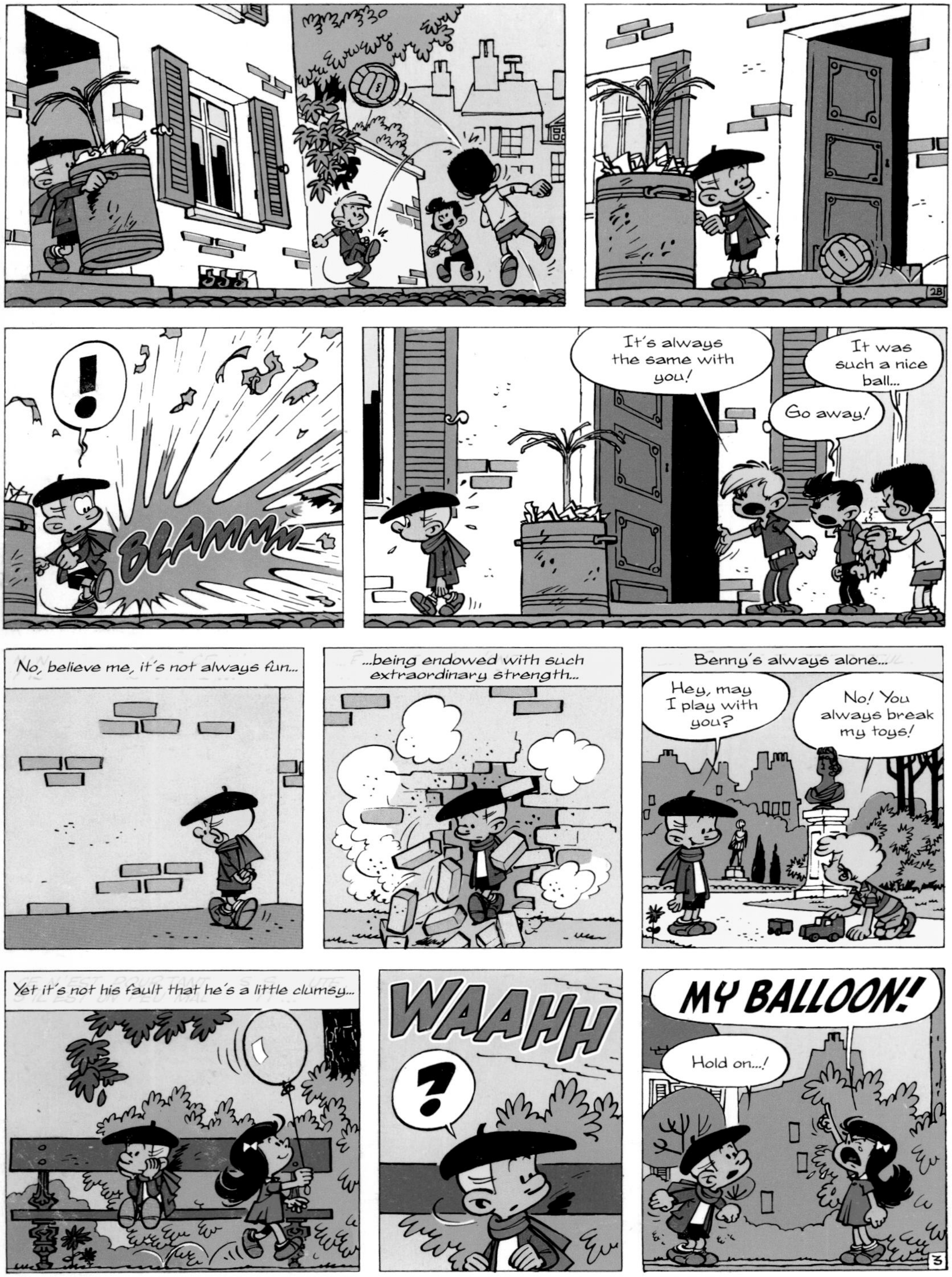
It's always the same with you!
It was such a nice ball...
Go away!
No, believe me, it's not always fun...
...being endowed with such extraordinary strength...
Benny's always alone...
Hey, may I play with you?
No! You always break my toys!
Yet it's not his fault that he's a little clumsy...
WAAHH
MY BALLOON!
Hold on...!

Will Benny be able to get the pink balloon back to the little girl? For the answer to that question, and much, much more—don't miss BENNY BREAKIRON #1 "The Red Taxis"—coming soon!